I:

MW00737301

To Elyse & David –
Honor the Earth!
Sally Bernankon

INDIAN ANNIE

A Grandmother's Story

SALLY AVERY BERMANZOHN

Bluejay Books

Indian Annie: A Grandmother's Story
by Sally Avery Bermanzohn

© 2017, Sally Avery Bermanzohn
All Rights Reserved

Printed in the United States of America

ISBN: 978-0692912522
Library of Congress Control Number: 2017947136

Bluejay Books
PO Box 373
Rosendale, NY 12472
sallybermanzohn@gmail.com

Cover drawing by Leola Bermanzohn

Feather image by Darren Pullman, 123RF.com

Cover design and author photo by Brent Robison

to all my relations

Contents

Advance Praise

"Spellbinding. Tears flowed as I became engrossed in the story of Indian Annie—her trial, tribulations and wisdom as she lived through the 19th century in the hills of Alabama where Indians were constantly in danger. This is a work that must be passed along, beginning in high school, to all those moving through life."
                    –Terry Leroy, Retired Reading Teacher Leader,
                                    Kingston City School District

"The conventional wisdom has it that after the 1830 Indian Removal Act, there were no more Indians east of the Mississippi. Yet Indian groups continually popup in the most unexpected places. Using creative strategies, they managed against the odds to hold onto their ancestral homelands. Sally Bermanzohn's story of a Chickasaw family refusing to move from their Alabama home is an example of Indian determination to remain put."
                    –Dr. Heriberto Dixon, Saponi Tribal Nation of Ohio,
                                    historian, storyteller, distinguished elder

"A heart-warming weaving together of stories from the oral tradition of her family with researched historical events. Sally Bermanzohn helps us to imagine what it must have been like for one family to come to terms with cultural interaction, bigotry, prejudice, hatred, fear, violence, compassion and love. Her words stitch together the emotions that come from the need to survive and perse-vere."

–Kay Olan, Mohawk Storyteller

"*Indian Annie* is a rare and precious gem, a slice of American history seen through the eyes of a Chickasaw elder. It is a story that reveals that, to survive, a people can be forced to abandon aspects of their culture, even as the survival of their souls depends upon preserving it. Those of African ancestry may feel comforted by the respect for the land, talking to the plants, understanding dreams to be real, and the honoring of the ancestors. For so many of us raised in cultures that suppress our traditions, this story is a healing elixir. Sally Bermanzohn understands the impor-tance of keeping alive the ways of the ancestors."

–Dr. Seshat, author of *Healing Across the Dimensions: Transformation through Spirit*

Ancestral Homelands
of the Chickasaw, Choctaw, Creek, and Cherokee Nations in the Deep South

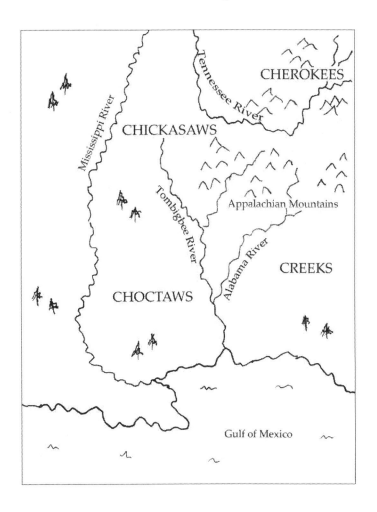

Deep South of the United States
after Indian Removal of the 1830s

Arkansas

Nashville

Tennessee

← To Oklahoma
(Indian Territory)

Memphis

Florence

Tennessee River

Freedom
Hills

Georgia

Natchez Trace

Andrew Jackson's Military Road

Birmingham

Mississippi River

Alabama

Mississippi

Florida

Louisiana

New Orleans

Gulf of Mexico

Family Tree

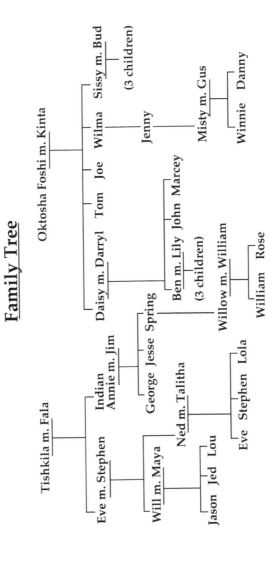

Tishkila m. Fala

Oktosha Foshi m. Kinta

Eve m. Stephen

Indian Annie m. Jim

Daisy m. Darryl   Tom   Joe   Wilma   Sissy m. Bud

(3 children)

George   Jesse   Spring

Jenny

Will m. Maya

Ned m. Talitha

Ben m. Lily   John   Marcey

Misty m. Gus

Jason   Jed   Lou

Eve   Stephen   Lola

(3 children)

Willow m. William

Winnie   Danny

William   Rose

Introductory Note, by Ned Ridge, Scribe

Freedom Hills, Alabama, September 1890

This is Indian Annie's story. She is my aunt. She and I sat under the oak tree in front of her house, and I wrote down what she said, word for word. It took all summer.

My family is Chickasaw, one of the tribes driven out of our ancestral homeland during Andrew Jackson's Indian Removal in the 1830s. Most Chickasaws trudged to Oklahoma in a trail of tears. But my family stayed in northwest Alabama, hidden in the mountains called Freedom Hills.

Indian Annie was a young'un in those removal years. Everyone had to give up their Chickasaw names and take on American names. The family called my mother "Eve" and her sister (my aunt) "Annie." They called my other aunts and uncles Wilma, Darryl, Tom, Joe, and Sissy.

While our elders were figuring out how to survive by "becoming white," little Annie declared that she was "proud to be an Indian." She always was hardheaded, my relatives said, and they nicknamed her "Indian Annie."

Now it is 1890, sixty years later. When my mother died last winter, and my aunt became our village's oldest elder. I feared that when Indian Annie passed, many of our family stories would die with her. I've known my aunt my whole life, because she and my mother lived next door to each other. She still delights in calling me a "whippersnapper," even though I am a schoolteacher in my forties.

Indian Annie speaks Chickasaw and English fluently, though she never learned to read or write. As long as I can remember, she has been the main storyteller in our village. She taught us Chickasaw history, and lessons for living in this world. She has no problem telling a story. The big challenge was getting her to let me put her words on paper. She made me promise I would write down only her words, instructions I've faithfully followed.

Every morning, I would find my aunt sitting in her rocking chair outside her log house, deep in meditation. She is thin, muscular, stooped with age. Her brown leather face reflects years working in the sun. Two long braids fall over her shoulders. Her hands are wrinkled, yet still powerful. Her voice ranges from soft and sweet to strong and angry. She often uses her hands, and sometimes waves both arms, as she expresses herself.

My aunt and I developed a routine. I slept in my mother's empty house. In the early morning, I would find my aunt sitting with her eyes closed, her body alert. She would be thinking about what she would say that day. I would sit quietly until she opened her eyes. Then I would give her a mug of tea that I made from nettle and mint leaves. We would sip tea, and listen to the birds and the bugs. Then, when she was ready, I would read to her what I had written down the day before. She would approve or correct it. That done, Indian Annie would close her eyes again. When she opened them, she was ready to continue telling her story.

1.

Birth of a Granddaughter

I am a Chickasaw elder. When I was a child, my family named me Annie because we needed "white" names. But my family calls me Indian Annie because I love our Indian ways of living, and I am stubborn.

In my long life, I've experienced much joy. And great pain, especially the deaths of my children. Another great loss was my own decision to give up my little granddaughter. It haunts me every day, giving away my precious Willow. Thank goodness for my family and my village – they pulled me through.

My granddaughter's birth — I remember it so clearly. It was in this very house, many years ago. Dawn seeped through the cracks of my log cabin. Lying there between the dream world and the day, I opened my eyes. My daughter, Spring, slept next to me, her belly huge with child.

Creeping out of bed, I pulled on my warm cloak. The cold winter was over, but mornings continued to be chilly. A small curl of smoke rose from the fireplace. I put dried sticks on the dying coals, and blew on the embers to restart the fire. This house once had two beds, a table and benches, all here in this room. Five of us lived here: my husband and me and our three children. But now only me. Over the years, the old bed broke and so did two benches. No one needed them, so they became firewood, and got me through some chilly nights.

My daughter snored gently. Slipping into my old deer-skin moccasins, I pushed the door open and stepped outside. Cold air greeted me, no longer icy. Pulling my cloak around me, I gave thanks for all that's been given to us.

My sister lived in the log cabin next door, a few steps away. There she and her husband raised their sons, Will and Ned. Next to them is the home that Will, their older son, built after he married Maya. Will and Maya raised their three children there. Our three little square houses, all in a row, all still here. They are made of logs, with mud plastered in between to keep out rain and cold. This is the traditional way we make our homes. In the old days, people thatched the roofs, but now we use wood shingles, which last longer and are safer. We built a stone fireplace and chimney into the wall on one side of the house, for cooking and warmth in winter. Outside is a fire pit and benches that we use in the warm weather.

Our gardens and fields spread out in front of our houses. Beyond the fields, the rocky ridge of the mountain rises up towards the sky. A stream travels down the ridge, across the fields, and through our village. We live close to this stream, near its life-giving waters. On the other side of the stream are more log houses, belonging to the other families in our village. We are all cousins, related through my mother and her sister who found this place.

We grow many kinds of vegetables and herbs. We

women are in charge of the farming. Each household has a kitchen garden for their immediate family. Behind these gardens is the field for our major crops—corn, beans, pumpkins, and squash. The women's council, which includes all the women of our village, decides what to plant to meet our needs. We women argue about the farming. My cousin, Wilma, thinks we plant too much. She says farming is too much hard work, and that we should get the men to hunt more animals to feed us. But Eve and I like the hard work of farming, and we like to plant enough so that we can get through the year, whether the men have good hunts or not.

The men work with us several times a year. They help us to clear the fields, plant the seeds, and harvest the crops. We share the work so that we all can eat. Mother Earth provides us with all we need.

Looking across our farm, I felt grateful. We'd survived the winter and it was the time of rebirth. The dawn's light spread through the field, waking up the plants and animals. My body ached for the return of warm weather.

I heard my sister moving inside her house, stoking her fire. I whistled to her softly and she beckoned me in. Quietly, I sat on the bench next to the fire, and she handed me a mug of nettle tea. Across the room, her husband continued to sleep.

"How's Spring?" she whispered.

"She's due now, in the Spring Equinox."

A door squeaked, and Spring stepped out of my house. We went outside and watched her, as she stretched and greeted the day. The sunlight fell on her long dark glossy hair. Seeing her, my heart filled with joy.

"Something's happening," Spring said, rubbing her back. "So much pressure. A cramp woke me up."

"We're ready for the birth," said Eve. "Water's heating for you, and soon I'll go and get Sissy."

Sissy grew up in our village. She followed in her mother's footsteps and became a midwife. She was always handy and available to help our families through many happy birthings, and sad ones too. Then she married a white farmer and moved to his farm over yonder. Now, when the labor pains come, someone has to go and fetch Sissy.

As Eve headed for Sissy's farm, I called to her, "Bring some fresh cream from Sissy's cow, to ease Spring's cramps."

Yes, the baby was coming. Through the day, off and on, Spring got her pains. Worry crept into my body. Keep busy, I told myself. Gather rags and wash them. Make tea. Spring walked around, groaning sharply every once in a while. She headed out for the field. "Don't get out of ear shot," I called to her. "Raspberry tea will be ready soon."

The best comfort for women is raspberry tea. I went to the wild raspberry bushes behind my house, and pulled off the tiny buds, just beginning to sprout in the sunshine. Water steamed in a pot hanging in my fireplace. When it simmered, I took the pot off the flame and added the fresh raspberry sprouts to steep. Good thing I had dried raspberry leaves from last summer, and could add them to the pot. After the tea steeped, I filtered out the leaves with a tea basket, glad that there was enough for a several mugs of tea.

My hands shook as Spring appeared from the cornfield and took the tea from me. Unlike me, my daughter was calm. Even my voice sounded shaky as I told her that Sissy was bringing some fresh cream for her tea.

The sun was low in the sky when Eve arrived with

Sissy. Springs's labor pains were coming more frequently. Sissy told us to prepare for a long night, since it was Spring's first birth.

Fear gripped me as darkness fell, memories of the happy drama of Spring's birth, and that of my two sons before her. But the sad times also haunted me. My first baby, born dead, and another one I birthed only to die the next day. Even more terrible memories came. One winter ago, my niece, Jenny, died in childbirth. Jenny was near the same age as Spring. They were best friends, both lanky and strong. How could Jenny die?

As night closed in on us, Sissy hovered over Spring, I felt tears filling my eyes. I wanted to help my daughter. Instead I was crying.

"Out!" said Sissy, looking me straight in the eye. "Go." Sissy ordered me out of my own house! I left obediently.

Grandmother Moon, big and full, looked down on our village. Under her light, I calmed down and wandered through the village. The children and men slept, but the women were awake. The mothers were keenly aware of the drama going on in my house.

Deer grazed in the moonlight on the edge of our fields, a good omen. We rarely saw deer. They had been hunted so hard that few were left.

A door opened, and my niece, Marcy, called me into her warm home. She pampered me, gave me squirrel broth to drink, made me lie down. I fell asleep.

Next thing I knew, my sister shook me. "Annie come! Quick!"

I jumped up, and Eve hustled me home. Sissy opened the door with a big smile. "Congratulations Grandma!" she said.

There lay my daughter with a happy exhausted smile,

and a baby girl in her arms. "Meet your granddaughter, " said Spring. "I want to name her Willow."

The next morning, Spring and I sat in our cozy house as she nursed her baby. Then she wrapped the little one in a cloth and placed her in my lap. I held the baby, so Spring could stretch her legs and wander through the village.

I sat there singing lullabies to the precious bundle on my lap, so soft and warm and beautiful. "Willow," I whispered, getting used to the sound. A stand of black willows grew next to our stream near the place we filled our water jugs. Willows are pretty trees, well rooted, with strong flexible trunks. Willow — a good name for this little girl, I thought to myself. I whispered, "Chishanko toba," which means Willow in Chickasaw.

She will need both strong roots and flexibility to live in this world, I mumbled to myself. The Indian Removal had taken away so many Native people from this land, and the Civil War had killed even more.

The Chickasaw word "nittaki" came to me. It means "early in the morning," a time of new beginning. I imagined this little one growing up in our village, part of our family's rebirth.

2.

Indian Removal

According to the white man's way of counting years, I was born in 1819, right here in this house. Tishkila was my mother. My father was the wounded Cherokee she fell in love with.

A happy child, I would run everywhere, flapping my arms. I would fall down, pick myself up, and keep running. The village gave me the spirit name of "Fochosh-oshi" which means duckling. They said I looked like a baby duck trying to fly off the pond.

Then the village gave us American names. I was Annie.

Eve, my big sister, was born one spring before me. We had lots of cousins, the five children of my aunt and uncle: Daisy, Tom, Joe, Wilma and Sissy. Cousin Wilma, was born one moon before me. We were the same age but we never got along. Sissy, the youngest cousin, was born when I was ten years old. How I loved little Sissy! I played with her like she was my own baby.

When I was small, Mama made me a tiny medicine bag out of rabbit skin to hang around my neck. She found a small duck feather to put in it, along with bits of dry herbs and tobacco. Here is that same little leather bag, all these years later, still hanging around my neck.

In the summer we celebrated the Green Corn Ceremony. We built a sacred fire, and gave thanks to Mother Earth for all our crops. The men beat the drum and everyone sang and danced. In the cold weather we gathered around the fire, sang, and listened to stories. I loved to sing, and so did everyone in our village. Singing connects us to the spirits of the earth, and the spirits of our ancestors.

When I was seven winters old, I saw my mother truly angry for the first time. She and others in the village talked about "treaty-making" with the Americans. What was "treaty-making"? I asked her.

"Go ask to your father," she muttered, brushing me off. "I'm busy. Leave me alone."

Hurt by her sharp words, I looked for my father. He told me the Americans and the Chickasaws were holding treaty-talks. It was not going well. The Americans wanted *all* of the Chickasaw land, and wanted us to leave here and go west. That was why Mama, a village leader, was cross!

Papa was Cherokee, and he grew up on the shores of the Singing River, which the whites called the Tennessee River. Cherokees and Chickasaws both lived where he grew up, and Papa grew up speaking the languages of both peoples. He knew the old songs, and loved to sing them in his scratchy voice.

Papa taught us the history of all the Muskogee peoples—Choctaw, Chickasaw, Creek, and Seminole, as well as the history of his own Cherokee people. He told wonderful stories, and my village named him Fala, or Crow, because crows, with their noisy crackling voices, tell stories. I loved my Papa.

Papa loved me, and he would answer my questions. He explained that our tribes had made many treaties with the white men. But the Americans never kept their promises, and they kept demanding more and more land from us. "All our tribes are angry," Papa said, "Cherokees, Chickasaws, Creeks, and Choctaws, too.

"Many Indians help the settlers," he explained. "The Chickasaws run ferries, so white people, as well as Indians, can get across the rivers. A ways north of here is the place where the Natchez Trace crosses the Tennessee River, and people need a ferry to get across. People called it Colbert's Ferry after Chief Tootemastubbe, whose white name is George Colbert. He and his brother Chief Itawamba, or Levi Colbert, made places called 'stands' for the settlers and Indians to eat and sleep along the Natchez Trace.

"Those Colbert Chickasaws got rich by ferrying the white people," Papa continued. "They bought slaves, and lived like rich white men. But most Indians were poor."

Papa explained that when he was growing up, all the young men were angry. Their tribes had lost land to the whites, and deer had been over-hunted, disappearing in many places. The youthful warriors could no longer hunt enough deer for their families to survive the winter.

"Many of us young braves looked to Tecumseh, the Shawnee warrior, who called on all tribes to unite against the white man. We called ourselves Red Sticks. But we got beat bad in the Creek War." Papa sighed, "Most of my friends were killed. I was lucky to survive. Andrew Jackson was the American general, and he pit Indians against each other. He promised tribes who supported him that that they could live here in peace forever. Of course Jackson did not keep his promises, and took more land away from our peoples. It was all part of their strategy of divide and conquer. "

Papa taught me all this history by talking to me. Even though I never learned to read, my bones absorbed the stories of the Indians. My father said storytelling was the *best* way to learn. I asked him questions, and he told me what he knew. Then he asked me questions to see what I had learned.

"What have you learned about 'treaty-making'?" my father asked me.

"The white man lies!" I blurted out. "He is greedy. He wants all our land."

"Very good!" said Papa. "You understand. That means you can learn — and teach — our history."

"Yes." I said, standing tall and stomping my foot, "We are *Indians!* We will not leave our mountain!"

"Okay, 'Indian Annie'," said Papa.

And that's how I got my name.

The first time I saw a white man, I ran in fear to my parents. The strange looking man came into our village with a group of Cherokees.

"Don't be afraid, my little one," my father said. "He is white, but he is with our Cherokee relatives. He married a cousin of mine and he is family."

Then my mother explained, "If a white men courts one of our women, she decides whether or not she wants to marry him. If he is respectful of our ways, then the marriage is welcomed, and that man may be adopted into our tribe."

Papa looked at Mama with a sly smile and said, "The white man says 'Indian women are bossy.'"

"Yes," my mother said, proudly lifting her head up and looking at me. "Indian women have a lot of say over things. Our houses and children belong to us, and we are the ones who decide how we farm. Most white men think *men* should make all the decisions. But some white men liked strong Indian women. They married into our tribe, and became part of our people."

Several years later, I was old enough to understand much of the grownup talk about the white men voting Andrew Jackson to be president. Jackson promised to "remove the Indians." He made the 1830 Indian Removal Law that said we had to leave our homelands, and go west to a place called "Indian Territory" or Oklahoma.

"How can they buy or sell our Mother Earth?" Papa asked. "We do not see the earth as something you can sell. But the whites have so many guns and coins and people to force the point and sway things their way." One summer, we traveled several days east to visit my father's Cherokee relatives. I remember them crying when we left, and we never saw them again. The American soldiers rounded up the Choctaws, Creeks, Chickasaws, and Cherokees, and made them walk west into the unknown to Oklahoma. It was the Trail of Tears. Many trails, many tears.

Our Chickasaw chiefs wanted us all to remove to Oklahoma, which means "Red People" in Choctaw. Our chiefs wanted us together to start a new life. We respected our chiefs, and knew that they had done what they could to stop the removal. But my parents refused to leave. So did everyone in our village, including us young'uns. We decided to stay, 'cause we belong to our mountain here in our sacred homeland.

We stayed because our elders thought we would be safe in the thick forests, rough ridges, hills and hollers. These mountains are not easy to travel through. Folks around here called this area Freedom Hills, because Indians hid here from the Removal. Decades later, it became Freedom Hills again during the Civil War, when young men hid out here to avoid fighting for the Confederacy.

As the years passed, we heard sad stories of our peoples trudging all the way to Oklahoma. So many people died on the way, especially the babies and the elders. Our older cousins, Tom and Joe, grew up here with us. But they married two Chickasaw sisters, and went west with their family. When Tom came back to visit us years later, he told us that they and their wives had survived the trip, but his wife lost the baby she was carrying, as well as her mother and aunt. Tom also told us that it was rough in Oklahoma, because so many tribes were forced to move there.

Some Indian people who stayed here in Alabama and Mississippi were found out, arrested, and sent west to Oklahoma. It was "illegal" for them – and for us — to live here in our homeland.

In those removal years, I asked my father, "Why are we so lucky to be in a place we can stay!"

"Because we are hidden here deep in the mountains," Papa said. "Your mother and your aunt found this spot. It's been a good place to hide, to grow our food, and live our traditions. But we still need to be careful."

"Tell me that story of finding this place," I asked.

"Oh no," he said, "That is a story your mother needs to tell."

I had to wait a long time for my mama to tell her story. It was summer, and there was too much work to be done.

"Wintertime is story-telling time," she told me. "Cold weather is when the elders tell their important stories."

I said, "Mama, I can't wait that long." She told me that I needed to develop patience.

It was the Moon of Cold Winds, when my sister, my cousins, and I finally got to hear the story of our village. We huddled together next to the fireplace in my aunt's log house to find how my mother and my aunt found this place.

3.

Tecumseh and Pushmataha

My mother and her sister grew up southwest of here in a Chickasaw town on the banks of the Tombigbee River, in the middle of the Chickasaw Nation. They were in the Bird Clan. My mother was named Tishkila, which means Bluejay. Bluejays are known to warn against danger, and to be hardheaded. Her sister was named Oktosha Foshi, which means Snow Bird or Chickadee, the small gentle birds, strong and resourceful in the winter cold.

As Tishkila and Oktosha Foshi grew to adulthood, they heard about a Shawnee named Tecumseh. He was a warrior from the lands far north of here. He called on all the tribes to unite against the Americans.

Two winters before the Americans killed Tecumseh in the War of 1812, my mother and aunt witnessed the great debate between Tecumseh and the Choctaw Chief Push-mataha. It was an experience that changed their lives. The story of their trip made me want to become a storyteller, to learn and teach our people's history.

Many Chickasaws lived along the Tombigbee River. Flat fertile land stretched out from the Tombigbee to the east and to the west. Women grew corn, beans, and squash there, as well as many other vegetables and herbs. Before the white man's deerskin trade killed off our animals, men hunted deer, bear, wolves, and many other animals in the surrounding forests.

There were other tribes nearby, and many spoke Muskogee languages, and could understand each other. The Choctaws lived to the south and the Creeks to the southeast. The Cherokees, who spoke a different language, lived further east towards the big ocean.

Sometimes there would be conflicts between the tribes, but usually they lived in peace before the white man came. We have good traditions for resolving conflicts and making plans. When there is a problem, a council is called to discuss all sides of the matter, and to try and make decisions with everyone's agreement. If it is a local issue, it is handled by a village council. The women's council makes the farming decisions. If there is a big issue – like war – a national tribal council is called. Our traditions allowed us to be truly free, because even if a national council comes to an agreement to go to war, each man or woman can still decide for themselves what they want to do.

After the pale-skinned people crossed the big ocean, our people faced bigger problems. The Chickasaws lived far enough west, so for a long time, our ancestors did not see the white men. They heard terrible stories about the diseases and bloodshed the whites brought. After a while, these pale face newcomers started coming over the mountains to where we live. First it was just a few men who wanted to trade with the Chickasaws and our neighboring tribes. Some white men married into our tribe. But then more and more whites came, and there were wars.

White men fought against white men. The ones who called themselves English, fought against the white men who were called French. They called us Indians, no matter whether we were Chickasaw, or Yamasee, a people who lived near the ocean. The English and French each tried to get our people to fight on their side against their enemy. The French befriended the Choctaw, and got them to fight against us Chickasaws, because we were trading with the English. This led to many wars between the Chickasaws and the Choctaws, even though we are cousins.

Tribal councils were called to discuss warfare. Councils lasted many days, and made many decisions. But the Europeans still managed to get Indians to fight against each other. When the American Revolution came, English were fighting against English who started calling themselves Americans, which is what they used to call us. These whites talked and dressed alike, and both worshipped Jesus Christ. But they hated one another.

The Chickasaw Council decided to stay neutral in the American war against the English. But each person could make up his or her own mind. Some Chickasaws fought for the English, others for the Americans, and others did not take sides.

My mother and my aunt were born in the early days of the new United States of America. George Washington was the president, and he signed peace treaties with the Chickasaws and many other tribes. In these Hopewell Treaties, the Americans promised to honor us, and our land. But they broke the treaties almost as soon as they signed them. White people came here, some respectful, but most acting like our land belonged to them.

The Americans cut down beautiful tall trees, saying this was "improving" the land. They built towns and so-called "trading posts" on our lands. My mother told a story about her father taking her to the American trading post in the Chickasaw Nation. Oh, the wonderful shiny things she saw in that store! But it was a trick. At first our people thought the trading post was generous. "You don't need to pay now," the Americans said. But they kept a tally of what you "bought," and the amount got bigger and bigger. The Americans made Indian people go into "debt," something our people never had heard of. The Americans said the only way the Chickasaws could pay off the debt was to sell our land to their government! In the white man's year of 1805, they got the Chickasaw chiefs to "sell" them most of our nation's land – mainly to settle the Chickasaw debts at the trading post.

As Tishkila and Oktosha Foshi grew up there was much talk of war. The English army threatened to crush the United States, even though the Americans had defeated them in the American Revolution. Indians were once again caught between warring white men. Some, like Tecumseh, sided with the English against the Americans. Others, like Choctaw Chief Pushmataha, saw Americans as friends. At the same time, the Red Sticks were fighting American settlers.

Our Chickasaw chiefs tried very hard to keep peace with the Americans. They wanted to avoid what happened in other places, like Ohio, Kentucky, and North Carolina, where the Americans were killing lots of Indians to get their land.

But Tecumseh called for all the tribes to unite against

the common foe – the Americans. Tecumseh had traveled with thirty warriors from the beleaguered Shawnee Nation, far north of here. They paddled in canoes as far south as they could, and then came by foot to the Choctaw Nation, a long journey.

Mushulatubbee, chief of the northern part of the Choctaw Nation, hosted Tecumseh and his men. Tecumseh told the chief that he wanted to speak to all the Choctaws. So Mushulatubbee called for National Council of the Choctaws, inviting the Chickasaws as well. The council was to be held on the shore of the Tombigbee River. Chief Mushulatubbee sent out runners in all directions to tell the people to come to the council.

The journey to hear Tecumseh was a great adventure for my mother and her sister. Chickasaw warriors, young and old, began their journey to the Council by canoe down the Tombigbee River. A few days later, Tishkila and Oktosha Foshi canoed with Chickasaw women elders. Because the Council location was downstream, they traveled with the current, and it only took two days paddling. The sisters enjoyed the excitement of the journey, traveling farther away from their village than they had ever been. Oktosha Foshi was especially excited because she fancied a certain young Chickasaw warrior.

The Chickasaw group, like all those traveling to the council, had prepared dried meat and ground corn meal for the trip, enough for nine or ten days. When they stopped to camp overnight, Tishkila and Oktosha Foshi gathered greens, roots, and berries to supplement their supper. They filled their water jugs from a spring so they would have fresh water to continue their journey.

When the sisters and their elders' canoe arrived at the council grounds, they paddled in behind other canoes.

Young warriors helped people beach their canoes. As Tishkila steadied the stern, a strong warrior gently helped the elders get out of their canoe. "Welcome!" he said in their language.

Then the warrior reached out his hand to help Tishkila get out of the canoe. For a moment, their eyes met.

"Tecumseh!" Another warrior called, and the strong man who had helped them left to join the other warriors.

"That was Tecumseh?" Tishkila asked Oktosha Foshi, "He was so kind!"

"Yes!" Said Oktosha Foshi, "That's why people love him."

As they walked into the council grounds, they saw hundreds of people, more people that they had ever seen in one place. The weather was warm, and people sat in groups scattered in a large field. Men wore bright blue or red shirts; the women wore dresses of calico cotton, decorated with ribbons and feathers. Some wore skins of deer and other animals. Warriors were dressed in breech clothes, some with dramatic red and black war paint covering their faces.

Then the Choctaw fire keepers lit a huge fire, a signal that people should gather for the council. Groups of warriors walked in and sat in circles around the blazing fire. The oldest warriors formed the central circle, leaving enough room for the speaker and his warriors. The middle-aged warriors sat behind the elders. The young warriors, with little experience, were in outer circles. Men and women who were not warriors, including Tishkila and Oktosha Foshi, sat in the outer-most circles.

Tecumseh entered with his warriors. He stood tall and strong, my mother told us, wearing a buckskin shirt, breechcloth, moccasins, and red headband. He gripped a

peace pipe in his hand showing that this would be a peaceful discussion, with respect to all assembled. People passed
their peace pipes around, each taking a puff.

Then Tecumseh addressed the crowd. He spoke
Shawnee, a language not understood by many in the
crowd. But everyone there understood every word he
spoke, because his translator spoke Choctaw clearly, with
the same power and drama as Tecumseh. The huge crowd
sat silently, listening to every word.

This is what my mother heard Tecumseh say:

"Where today are the Pequot? The Narragansett? The
Mohawks? Where are the many other once powerful tribes
of our race? They have suffered before the oppression of
the white men, as snow before a summer sun. Look over
their once beautiful country, and what do you see now?
Naught but the ravages of the pale-face destroyers. So it
will be with you Choctaws and Chickasaws!"

Tecumseh directly challenged the crowd: "Sleep not,
O Choctaws and Chickasaws in false security and delu-
sive hopes. Before the pale-faces came among us, we
enjoyed unbound freedom, had neither riches, wants, nor
oppression. How is it now? Wants and oppressions are our
lot; are we not controlled in everything? Are we not being
stripped day by day of the little that remains of our ancient
liberty? The annihilation of our race is at hand unless we
unite in one common cause against the common foe."

At this point, some of the younger warriors jumped up
and, with tomahawks raised, yelled war whoops. Oktosha
Foshi saw Naki, her beloved, among them. Tecumseh sig-
naled them to be quiet.

"If we remain apart and disunited, the whites will soon
conquer us all," Tecumseh continued. "And we will scatter
like the fall leaves before the wind. The bones of our dead

will be plowed up and their graves turned into fields. Soon your mighty forest trees will be cut down to fence in the land, which the white intruders dare to call their own. Soon the whites' broad roads will pass over the graves of your fathers. "

Tecumseh's words touched everyone there. He spoke truth. But then he said something that made Tishkila stop short. Tecumseh said, "War or extermination is our only choice." Tishkila felt a knot tighten in her stomach. She thought, *Are those the only choices? Must there be war?*

Tecumseh declared that if the tribes united, they could beat the Americans. He said they were "backed by the strong arm of the English army." My mother knew that the English had gotten Indians to fight against American Revolution. *And the English lost.* Why would it be different this time?

Tecumseh finished and sat down. The council went on, others speaking. But night was falling, and many left for their lodges to sleep. As Oktosha Foshi and Tishkila walked with their elders to their camp site, Oktosha Foshi whispered to her sister, "I'm gonna go see my Naki."

That night Tishkila quickly fell asleep. In the dawn's early light, she awoke for a moment, as her sister crawled next to her, under their blanket.

The following day, Choctaw Chief Pushmataha spoke against Tecumseh. He said Tecumseh's call to arms was "rash and dangerous." He warned of the consequences of "going to war when our own strength is unequal to the task." He emphasized the greater power of the Americans in arms, money, and people.

"What measures are best for us to adopt?" Pushmataha asked, admitting that the whites had wronged many tribes, but not yet the Choctaws. "The whites should *not* be forgiven for their wrongdoing, but if we try to destroy them, they will destroy us. The American people now are friendly towards us."

Pushmataha ended saying, "If there is war between the English and the Americans, *I will join our friends, the Americans.*"

Then Tecumseh jumped into the circle and declared, "All those who will follow me in this war, raise your tomahawks in the air above your heads!" And suddenly it looked like half the warriors assembled lifted their tomahawks up to support Tecumseh.

Then Pushmataha jumped into the circle, and shouted, "All those who will follow me to victory and glory in this war, let me see your tomahawks in the air." And the other half of the warriors raised their tomahawks above their heads.

The knot in my mother's stomach tightened. There's going to be war, she thought, and our people will be fighting each other!

Tishkila leaned over to talk to her sister, and found that Oktosha Foshi was no longer there. Tishkila looked for her through the crowd, and saw her talking to her warrior boyfriend, excited and proud.

The council continued as people tried to figure out how to resolve their deep divisions. But Tishkila and Oktosha Foshi had to leave with their elders to paddle back home.

The return was a harder, longer journey, because they needed to paddle upstream. For four days, Tishkila dug her paddle deep into the Tombigbee, over and over, paddling home against the current. She remembered that the Tombigbee was a Choctaw word for "coffin-maker." As she fought the strong current, she thought, *Why war? Why can't there be another way?*

4.

Tishkila and Oktosha Foshi Seek Another Way

The journey to hear Tecumseh was the most momentous experience of my mother and my aunt's lives. It raised the questions of what people should do when there seemed to be no good choices, only ways fraught with violence and hardship.

Though seeking to unite the tribes, Tecumseh's words had the opposite result. As the sisters paddled back to their Chickasaw village with their elders, they learned how fearful their elders were of opposing the Americans. When they got home, they learned that their town's chief had sided with Pushmataha against Tecumseh.

The conflict within the Choctaws increased after Tecumseh's speech. Chief Pushmataha declared that any warriors, who joined the Red Sticks and fought against the Americans, would be *executed* upon their return to the Choctaw Nation.

Several young Chickasaw warriors quickly left the area to join Tecumseh and the Red Sticks. Oktosha Foshi and Naki got married. But, because they admired Tecumseh, most in their town shunned them. Naki decided he needed to join his warrior friends in the Red Sticks.

It was hard times for Oktosha Foshi. She met secretly with her husband a few times after that. The War of 1812 began, and a winter later, the American army killed Tecumseh. Then General Andrew Jackson led American and Indian troops in the Creek War against the Red Sticks. In the Battle of Horseshoe Bend, in Alabama, the American army, joined by Choctaw, Chickasaw, and Cherokee warriors, killed something like 1400 Redsticks –men, women, and children. One of the dead was Naki, Oktosha Foshi's husband. Oktosha Foshi was distraught and furious at every Chickasaw who sided with the Americans.

Jackson became the hero in the eyes of the white Americans. But Indians around here hated him. After the war was over, Andrew Jackson forced the Indians nations–including those who had fought under his command–to give up precious land.

Tishkila stood by her sister, and they both felt isolated in their town. The war divided family against family. Their family was very small, since their mother had died years earlier. The one person they trusted was their mother's close friend, a medicine woman who lived alone upstream of the town. Alikchihoo means woman doctor, and for many years, she had been teaching the sisters about medicine plants. Alikchihoo was someone Oktosha and Tishkila could confide in.

Then Tishkila had a nightmare. She and her sister were trapped in their village as the Americans burned it to the ground. When all seemed lost, Tishkila and Oktosha Foshi were suddenly flying up in the air where only birds can go. High in the mountains, they found a place that was beautiful and peaceful.

The next morning Tishkila told her dream to her sister. "Yes!" Said Oktosha Foshi. "We need to up and leave this place. We'll fly away! We're Bird Clan, we can do this."

It's true they were in the Bird Clan, like their mothers before them, and those of us who follow. Many of us were named after birds.

Oktosha Foshi (Chickadee) and Tishkila (Bluejay) talked to Alikchihoo about the dream, telling her they wanted to find a new place to live. After much discussion, Alikchihoo suggested they explore the hilly dense forest northeast of there, a good spot to live hidden. She suggested that the sisters paddle upstream with her in her canoe to the place where the river crosses the Chickasaw Path. Alikchihoo would visit her relatives up there while Tishkila and Oktosha Foshi explored. Then they could canoe back together.

They prepared for the journey, drying meat, making corn meal, packing herbs. They told their relatives that Alikchihoo was taking them on a trip to learn about medicine herbs. Then they paddled with her up the Tombigbee for two days, until it crossed the Chickasaw Path.

As they paddled, Alikchihoo gave them some wise advice. The Chickasaw Path was the fastest trail travel north to where they wanted go. But, she told them, the whites took over Chickasaw Path, and named it the Natchez Trace. "Now it's dangerous to travel on it," said Alikchihoo, "because of the thieves."

The Natchez Trace went from the Gulf Coast to the big town they call Nashville. "Some folks call the Natchez

Trace the 'devil's backbone' because of all the evil people who travel it," Alikchihoo told them. "That's why people travel in groups. You will see fancy men on horses. You will see poor men called Kaintucks, who farm up north in places called Kentucky and Ohio. They bring their livestock and crops down the Mississippi on a river barge to market. After they sell everything, they walk all the way home, which is a long way north of here. You will know who the Kaintucks are 'cause they look and smell horrible."

Seeing the sister's determination and fear, the medicine woman gave them exact instructions. "Safest way to travel is to start at the crack of dawn. No talking while walking! Listen carefully so you can hear horses or people, and you have enough time to find a hiding spot before they get to you."

As they were leaving, Alikchihoo gave them ten sticks. "Break one of these every day, and plan your travel so that you will be back at this spot in ten days. I'll meet you then right here, and we'll travel back home down the Tombigbee."

Tishkila and Oktosha left their trusted friend, and nervously waded to the shore of the Tombigbee River where the old Chickasaw Trail, renamed the Natchez Trace, crossed it. The river was shallow enough to walk through the water to the place where the trail continued. The Natchez Trace was well used, wide enough for three or four people to walk side by side. Human footsteps had padded down the earth so it was like walking in a smooth riverbed. Trees grew on both sides, tangled branches overhead.

The sisters followed Alikchihoo's advice, walking silently, listening intently for any human sounds on the road. The first day, they saw no other people, only birds, squirrels, rabbits, chipmunks, and three deer. They walked until the sun went behind the tall trees, then they left the Trace to find a place in the forest to spend the night. They ate their dried food, rolled up in their blanket, and quickly fell asleep.

Before dawn the next day, they woke up and continued traveling north on the Trace, as fast as they could walk. The sun was overhead when they heard noise approaching them from behind. Quickly they left the trail, climbing up a rocky wooded hill. There they watched as a scruffy, dirty, group of exhausted-looking white men lumbered by. One, who looked even whiter than a pale-skin, was riding a mule, tied on to it so he wouldn't fall off. These were the Kaintucks that Alikchihoo had told them about.

After the Kaintucks passed, the sisters rested in their rocky hideout. They cautiously looked eastward across the Trace and through the forest. They saw more thick forest and steep hills. Tishkila whispered, "That looks like what we want. We need to continue along the Natchez Trace until we see a stream going east that we can follow."

Soon they left the Trace, following a creek eastward. Walking all that afternoon, they saw no signs of humans. As the sun went down, they felt safe enough to look for herbs and berries to eat. That evening they bathed in the creek, and went to sleep early.

The next day they found a narrow path next to the stream that had deer scat on it. A deer trail, a good sign. They followed the trail as it went higher into the hills. Lots of hills, rocks, and thick forest surrounded them. They walked next to rocks that went straight up, higher than a man standing on a man's shoulders.

Suddenly Tishkila stopped. The deer path continued

in front of them, but Tishkila felt the spirit of her dream telling her to leave the path and go upwards. "There," Tishkila said to Oktosha Foshi, pointing up the wall of rocks. "We need to go up *there*." Like in her dream, it was a place where only birds could go.

"But how?" asked Oktosha Foshi. They looked around until they found a place where they could pull themselves up, grabbing tree roots in the rocks. They were young and nimble, and climbed carefully to the top of the rocks. They walked into the thick forest, and saw sunlight through the trees. Following the light, they walked out into a beautiful meadow with a steep mountain ridge beyond it.

Tishkila paused and looked around the cabin at me and my cousins. "This is what I dreamed!" She cried, holding out her arms to all of us.

"And that is how we found this place where we are sitting right now!" said Oktosha Foshi.

I looked around. It was dark outside, and we could hear the cold wind blowing. It was cozy and warm inside my aunt's cabin, and most of my cousins had fallen asleep. Wilma was snoring loudly. But I was wide-awake. My mother and aunt's story excited me, made me want to be a storyteller like them.

I asked them, "What happened next?"

5.

Building a Hidden Village

Realizing I truly wanted to hear her stories, my mother began answering any question I asked her. I was getting big, almost as tall as she was. We talked while we worked, bringing in water, gathering wood, washing clothes, hoeing, planting, harvesting.

"Oktosha Foshi and I built this village from scratch," she told me. "We found everything we needed to survive right here."

Then she laughed, saying, "We even found husbands, and raised you children."

When they found this place, Tishkila and Oktosha Foshi stayed a few days, eating the dried foods they brought with them. They also picked berries, herbs, and sassafras roots to eat. They swam in the stream, and found the mountain spring with its clear drinking water.

They explored all around the meadow, and climbed the rocky ridge. From the peak, they could see the green forest-covered hills and hollers, stretching out in front of them in all directions. There was no sign of pale-faced people, or any other human beings. They thought, "This is the place!"

On the tenth day, Oktosha Foshi and Tishkila arrived back at their meeting place where the Natchez Trace crossed the Tombigbee River. They found Alikchihoo waiting for them. They canoed with her back down the Tombigbee to their town. They told only a few close relatives about their secret place.

One moon later, Oktosha Foshi and Tishkila returned with several trusted cousins who helped them build a shelter. They chose a spot near the stream, and built a one-room log cabin to keep them warm in winter. They cleared a small field where Oktosha Foshi and Tishkila could plant corn and vegetables. The spot was safe because the only way a person could get there was on foot, if they knew the way and could climb up rocks.

That's how our village began. Oktosha Foshi and Tishkila lived out their lives here. A few others joined them. First was a Chickasaw man, Kinta, who knew how to build log homes. Oktosha Foshi fell in love with him, and they had children. A wounded Cherokee came to the village looking for peace. They named him Fala, and he won Tishkila's heart, and that's how Eve and I came into this world.

My Aunt Oktosha and Chief Kinta had five children, who are my cousins: Daisy, Tom, Joe, Wilma, and Sissy. My mother and Fala had only two children who survived: Eve and me. We were born during the treaty-making years, and grew up during the removal years. The boy cousins, Tom and Joe, both married Chickasaw girls, and removed to Oklahoma with their families. Daisy, Wilma, Sissy, Eve and I all stayed here, grew up, and had children. We all still live in the village, except Sissy who stays put over yonder with Bud, the white farmer she married.

Jim, a Choctaw man, courted me, and we had so much fun. That was almost fifty years ago, but it feels like yesterday. One afternoon, during the Corn Moon, Jim and I were walking through our fields. Jim was so handsome, and I couldn't stop looking at him. We came to the place where the cornfield ended and the meadow stretched towards the ridge.

Jim said to me, "Run!"

I said, "Why?"

"'Cause I want you to!"

So I ran, and Jim ran after me. I could run fast, but he was faster. He grabbed me, and we both rolled onto the soft meadow ground.

"I caught you. That means you have to marry me!" he laughed. "It's an old Choctaw custom." And I laughed and hugged him.

Then Jim looked serious. "I love you even though you're Chickasaw."

"What do you mean? I'm proud of being Chickasaw!"

Jim sat up, a serious expression covering his face. "Choctaws and the Chickasaws used to be the same people," he said.

"I know. I learned the story of the two chiefs, Chahta and Chikasa, when I was a child," I said.

"I bet your Chickasaws didn't teach the rest of the story," Jim frowned. "Do you know that when the English came, the Chickasaws became slavers for them? The English wanted slaves – Indian slaves – to do the hard farming work. So those greedy Chickasaws hunted their own cousins–my people. They forced Choctaws to be slaves and sold them to the English!"

"No, I didn't know that." I paused and glanced at Jim. Just a few minutes ago, he had been so friendly.

"Wait," Jim frowned, "I haven't finished my story. The Choctaws sided with the French, and went to war against the Chickasaws. But then the English kicked the French out, and then the Americans kicked the English out. And now the Americans have kicked the Indians out. And the Choctaws and Chickasaws have become friends again."

"But," he added with a frown, "some Choctaws still harbor bad feelings against your tribe."

"I apologize for the wrongs of my ancestors against yours," I said seriously.

We sat there in the quiet. With my heart pounding, I whispered, "Are you sure you want to marry a Chickasaw girl?"

"Well," said Jim, "This is beautiful land. And it is good that your village still keeps traditions."

Hmmm, I thought, felling suddenly hurt... and wary of what Jim might say next.

Then that beguiling smile returned to Jim's face, "Oh, and I like you too. I *do* want to marry you." Once again I recognized the handsome young man who had just chased me across the meadow.

Trying to be serious, I said, "In the Chickasaw tradition, you will need to talk to my relatives."

So Jim talked to my mother and father, my aunts, and my sister. Jim said they "grilled" him. My mother told me they liked Jim. "He's honest, and he's a proud Choctaw," she said.

Jim and I married under the Harvest Moon, which is also called the Courting Moon. His Choctaw relatives came to our village for the ceremony. There were lots of comments and jokes about our tribes' history. To show that everyone was friends and family, our Choctaw and Chickasaw cousins together built us this log home. They did a good job. Here it is still standing.

Jim loved our village because we lived according to our traditions. Tishkila, my mother, and Oktosha Foshi, my aunt, were the respected elders who had the greatest say in everything our village did. Oktosha Foshi's husband was named Kinta, or beaver, in Chickasaw, because he was a builder. Kinta became our village chief because we needed someone who could communicate with the world outside the village. His job was to keep in touch with other pockets of Indians still here after the removal, and to make friends with whites if possible. Kinta was a good chief. He was friendly to all, and spoke English as well as Chickasaw. This was our tradition: the women ran the village, and the men kept watch on the outside world.

Even though we managed to stay here in our hidden village, the Indian Removal brought big changes to our lives. We were always on guard. Our parents decided we all had to learn to talk English, so people would consider us white. We gave up our Indian dress, the bright colors and patterns we liked for our clothes, and began wearing the same rough clothes as our white neighbors, the dull beige, the somber browns. But I kept wearing the medicine bag my mother made me, because it was small and I could tuck it under my shirt so no one could see it.

To this day, many whites in Alabama and Mississippi hate Indians. Since the removal, they say it has been "illegal" for Indians to live here. To them we are flaunting the law. South of here, the flatlands were a harder place for the Indians to hide. The whites moved into those lands, and some got rich making big plantations with slaves. This is what happened down along the Tombigbee River, where my mother and aunt were born.

Anyone who saw us working in our fields would think we were white farmers, with a deep tan from all that farming. Really, some of us weren't that much darker than the whites. Chickasaws have been marrying whites for some time, and we come in many different shades.

My father died soon after my marriage to Jim. I missed him so much. Mama told me it was good to mourn his passing, but that I should also be grateful for all that he taught me. My mother lived on for many years. I got closer to her, learned so many stories from her. And she taught me to talk to the plants, so I became a good farmer.

Gradually some white farmers moved into the valley down from our village and built small farms. Like us, they eke out a living in the meadows between the hills. We traded with them and made friends. Some of them became relatives, like the family that Sissy married into.

But it got harder to pass our way of life. Sissy, the midwife who helped with Willow's birth, is my cousin. She is Oktosha Foshi's youngest daughter, about ten winters younger than me. A full-blood Chickasaw, she grew up in this village and married a young white man, a good, respectful young farmer. But rather than follow the Chickasaw custom of bringing him to live with his wife's people, she went to live on *his* farm. He built her a big house, with four whole rooms, each one the size of my house. And there's a front porch with rocking chairs on it. Sissy is living like a white woman. It's not all bad. Sissy is a good midwife for the white and Indian women alike. And when she comes to see us, we talk Chickasaw. But she did not teach her children to speak Chickasaw, and they don't even seem to know they are Indian. That makes me sad.

In our village, we joke about the changes we have made to get along with these Americans. We laugh at white people in our own language, but only when we are by ourselves. No talking Chickasaw when white people are around! But I talk our language as much as I can. I think and dream in Chickasaw. Meanwhile, the younger ones seem to be forgetting how to talk the talk the old way. They are so anxious to talk to the world outside our village, they are forgetting how to talk to their own hearts.

To the outside world, we had become white. Outside our village, we used our paleface names, and I was just Annie. But I rarely went outside our farm and mountain. This village was my world. Here I remained Indian Annie.

6.

Motherhood

Eve got married two autumns before I did. She married Stephen, a Chickasaw who had become a Christian. Stephen learned some English, including the numbers. He wrote in this book he calls the Bible, our family's marriages and the births of our children. I have kept this book ever since.

1838: Eve marries Stephen

1839: Eve and Stephen's first child born, named Will

1840: Annie marries Jim

1842: Annie and Jim's first child born, named George

1843: Annie and Jim's second child born, named Jesse

1844: Annie and Jim's third child born, unnamed, died on 2nd day

1847: Annie and Jim's daughter born, named Spring

1849: Eve and Stephen's second child born, named Ned

These are the names of our children that were born alive. Eve and I had other babies that never breathed in this world. Stephen called them "stillborns" and did not write them down in the Bible. But Eve and I remember those little ones with our hearts. Eve lost three stillborns, and I lost one. Those were sad times. Yet we were very grateful for the five healthy children that we raised.

When Eve married Stephen, the village built them a house, just the way they built me and Jim a house a few years later. Eve and I lived next door to each other until she died last winter. Together we grew corn, beans, squash, sunflowers, pumpkins, and herbs. We dried crops to get us through the winter. Our five children, Will, Ned, George, Jesse, and Spring, grew up together, more like brothers and sister than cousins.

Note from Ned, the scribe:

Indian Annie then looked at me, saying, "You just got born. Share your early memories."

"But I am just the scribe," I said. "This is your story."

"Yes," said my aunt, "it is my story, but also yours. Your name is written down here in this Bible. 'Ned, born 1849.' What do you remember as a young boy?"

"Hmm." I thought for a while, and then said, "My first memory is trying to keep up with my big brother and my cousins. They would run away from me, and then laugh at me. They were so big, and I was so little. They teased me. Spring was almost as small as me. She was nice to me. I think she liked having someone small to play with.

"I remember holding hands with her as we jumped into the swimming hole where we bathed every day in the warm months. When winter came, Will, George, and Jesse would still jump in that cold water. But Spring and I put water for our baths in a bucket, so we could bring it back to clean ourselves in front of the fire, without having to get so cold. Spring and I also did our every-day chores together — fetching drinking water for our families from the spring, and gathering firewood.

"Aunt Annie, I remember you and my mama. You two were always together, farming in the fields in the early morning, sitting out under this tree in the mid-day, cooking meals and eating outside. Annie, I remember you singing Chickasaw lullabies to us every night. I remember my dad playing stickball with Will, George, Jesse, me, and our other cousins. I remember Dad and Uncle Jim taking us on hikes and teaching us about the forest and the spirits of the animals. We went on camping trips 'just for men', and our dads told us stories about Chickasaw and Cherokee warriors in times past."

"Write that all down in your notebook," said Annie. "It is part of the story."

Then Annie closed her eyes, as I wrote down my memories. I read what I wrote back to my aunt, and she bestowed her approval. The next day, Annie continued telling her story.

Ned "gets wet"

Now that Ned has given his voice to our story, I can tell a little a tale about him when he was young. Ned, that little whippersnapper, was the youngest of Eve's and my children. He was smart and curious.

Ned loved to hear the stories of our people. After my father died, I became our village storyteller. I spent a lot of time with Ned because he was the child most interested in our history.

Ned's father, Stephen, had become a Christian as a boy, and he had some schooling that taught him some English. Stephen said our village needed a person who could read the white man's words. We needed one of our children to learn how to read and write. We all agreed, and little Ned was the natural choice.

Stephen found a young Baptist minister a good hike

down from our village. Preacher Jones was white, an "Indian Lover", meaning he'd opposed the Indian Removal. Stephen joined the church, and the preacher told Stephen he needed a school-age assistant. Stephen introduced the preacher to his son, Ned. "If your son becomes a Baptist," Preacher Jones said, "I will teach him how to read and write."

So Ned began working with Preacher Jones. Ned has a beautiful singing voice, and he joined the church choir. Ned learned about Jesus Christ Our Lord, which he had to do in order to get baptized and become a member of the Church.

One day Eve came running over to me. "That husband of mine wants me to become a Christian!" Eve declared. "If I go to Ned's baptism, I'm likely to end up wet."

I opened my mouth to ask her what she meant by "getting wet." Did it mean that everyone took off their clothes to jump in the river?

Suddenly Ned and Stephen came through the door. "Auntie Annie," Ned said very sweetly, "Will you come to my baptism?"

"Will I get wet?" I asked.

"No," said Stephen. "You will just be a guest."

Before I could say a word, Eve said, "Good. That settles it. Annie will go instead of me. Just tell the preacher your mama is home 'cause she's sickly."

Cousin Daisy lent me her "Sunday-go-to-meeting" clothes, and that next Sunday morning we walked down yonder to that church. I took Spring with me, and I believe it was one of the first times she had been out of our village. And it was the first time for both of us to go inside a church. The preacher was friendly. The singing was real pretty, 'specially when Ned took a solo, and everyone shouted, "Hallelujah!"

Preacher Jones talked about sin, the devil, and Jesus. Then we went outside down to the riverside. And I learned what Eve meant by "getting wet." The preacher dunked Ned in the river–in his church clothes! Spring and I had to cover our mouths to keep from laughing out loud.

For years after that, Ned assisted Preacher Jones. And he learned how to read. Ned tried to teach me to read, but I couldn't learn it. All those scratchy little letters looked blurry to me. I couldn't tell them apart. But I could make out the numbers if they were written down big. Ned also taught me the English calendar. I liked the names of the seasons — winter, spring, summer, fall — that are just different words for our seasons.

But the whites' system of "months" made no sense to me. Ned told me some of those months are named after emperors, like July and August. The months have different numbers of days, some with thirty, others thirty-one, and one with only twenty- eight days. Moons are a much better way to count, because it's based on something we can see with our own eyes: Grandmother Moon as she gets bigger, then smaller. And there are thirteen moon cycles every year.

Those days, raising our children, were the best ones of my life. Our village thrived. Despite the removal, we had twenty people living here. Twenty-one if we included the old medicine man who lived alone on the ridge, and only came into the village when someone got sick.

We hoped our children would stay and live our way of life. We farmed the way our ancestors had taught us. Several white farmers moved into the valley down yonder.

They hired our young folks as farm labor. My sons, George and Jesse, learned American farming techniques, and we tried out some of them. But the whites, with their mules and plows, dig too deep into the soil, and they plant their seeds too close together. They plant the same crops in the same places year after year. This wears out the soil. Our ways are much better.

Our young folks told us about a farmers' market in Market Town, south of here, down the Military Road. It was a place to sell the excess crops we grew. Us older folks were skeptical, but our children were enthusiastic. "It's worth a try," I thought.

So early one morning during the Harvest Moon, we headed out to the farmers' market. Daisy and her husband, and me and my husband, went along with our sons. We pulled a cart full corn and squash, and each of us hauled a bag of beans on our backs. We walked down our hidden trail to where it met a bigger trail that led towards Preacher Jones' church. Then we followed a bigger trail down to the Military Road, built by that rapscallion Andrew Jackson, right after the War of 1812. That day was the first time I had stepped foot on that road. It was wider and straighter than any trail I'd ever seen, cutting right through the forest into the distance.

It took us a long time to walk down that road. That bag of beans on my back got heavier and heavier. Finally we got to a town, where all buildings rose up high from the ground. Why are the houses so high? I asked my husband who had been out in the world much more than me. "Oh," said Jim, "That's the way the whites build them. They got stair steps that you climb up to what they call 'the second story.'"

When we got to the market, people were already haggling over the price of vegetables. We saw farmers with good set ups – tables for the corn, potatoes, beans, and fruits, and chairs for the farmers to sit on behind their produce. I saw dark-skinned people hauling vegetables on their backs to a big farm stand at the front of the market. "Are they slaves?" I whispered to Jim. "Yup," he replied.

The only space for us was at the back of the market. There were no tables there. We put our bags on the grass. My son Jesse spread a cloth out for the corn and beans, and Daisy and I stacked them up real pretty. We sat there on the ground behind our vegetables, watching the people at the market. There were different kinds of folk there. Rich people with fancy clothes on, and elegant hats. "Don't think they ever get their hands dirty," Daisy said to me. The fancy folks stayed at the front of the market. They didn't even look our way.

I looked at everyone, searching for people who might be like us, hidden Indians. Most people there were regular looking white people, with rough hands and faces. They talked and laughed, enjoying the market. Then there were the dark-skinned folks, working hard and silent, with stern-looking white men watching them closely. I saw a family, a woman sitting there like me. Maybe they were Indian. I tried to catch her eye, but she looked away from me, afraid.

After a while, some folks came back where we were. "They're looking for deals," George whispered to me. I saw how my son bargained with them. He sold all the crops that we brought with us, and made us good money that day. I was proud of him. I thought to myself that he was on his way to becoming a good farmer, someone who could relate to all kinds, both Indians and whites.

I learned a lot that day. For one thing, I learned we were

poor — something never discussed in our village. I realized I didn't like going to that market. It made me tired.

On the other hand, my sons loved the market. It was an adventure. In the years that followed, our boys would go to the market with our excess crops. With the money they made, they bought tools, cloth, and things we needed to get through the winter.

Our young folks met other young people there. Since everyone in our village is cousins, our young'uns need to look elsewhere for marriage partners. When their little sister, Spring, got big enough to walk to Market Town and back, my boys loved to take her with them.

They didn't want me to go with them, because they said I "looked too Indian," and even worse, "*acted* too Indian." I told them I was proud of how I looked and acted, and didn't want to go the durn farmers' market, anyhow.

In those years before the Civil War, my mother was old and frail. I wanted to spend time with her. I fixed a bench in our garden so she could sit and teach me all she knew. I loved listening to the birds and the bugs with her, and singing to the plants. Every day something new happens in our garden. My mother pointed to the feathers of a blue jay and chickadee that were lying on the ground. She told me to put them in my medicine bag, to remind me of her and her sister, of Tishkila and Oktosha Foshi. "You come from a long line of women who love the earth," she told me. That made me feel good.

Both my mother and her sister passed into the spirit world in the years before the big war. Our Chief Kinta got old, and we knew he soon would leave us. Our village council decided he should train one of our young men to help him in his old age, and to learn from him. Eve's oldest, Will, was selected because he is thoughtful and good at working with people. So Will started traveling with Kinta when he visited with the other hidden Indians. When Kinta died our village elders chose Will as our new chief, even though Will was only twenty winters old.

Those were the good times. I loved Jim and our children, and our cousins, nieces, and nephews, our whole village. We were survivors, good at preparing for winter, and living through good times and bad. But there was one storm we weren't prepared for — the war between the north and south. We saw the thunderclouds in the distance, felt the shift in the wind. But there was to be no shelter in this world from that monstrosity they called Civil War.

7.

Civil War

The Civil War destroyed my family.

A war over slavery–about who is a slave, who is free, who gets rich, who stays poor. About who controls the land and the people.

When the English came to this land, they wanted slaves, lots of them, to grow tobacco, and later cotton, on giant plantations. That's how some of those whites got rich. At first the English made poor whites into slaves, called them "indentured servants." Then they enslaved Indians, then Africans.

My husband taught me about the Indian slave trade. How Chickasaw warriors hunted the Choctaws like they were animals, then sold these human beings to the English as slaves. But this slave trade was dangerous because the Choctaws fought back and killed lots of Chickasaws. This slave trade tore apart our tribes, killing thousands of people. Then came the Yamasee War. The Yamasees lived in the east next to the great ocean, and they led a rebellion of warriors from different tribes, and they killed hundreds of English.

The Yamasee War ended the Indian slave trade. Those snobby English were shocked that the Indians could unite and carry out such a rebellion. So the English stepped up the African slave trade. They brought more and more Africans from across the sea. The Africans, living breathing people like us, found themselves in bondage in a strange land. Those white men enslaved Africans for the same reason they took the land away from the Indians. That was how they got rich.

As my sons grew big, we heard talk about a war to keep the southern way of life. What they meant was they were ready to kill to keep their slaves. Most folks in these parts, white and Indian, did not like the idea of war. People said, "Why risk your life in a war so the rich can keep slaves?" We talked about it in our village, and I spoke my mind. Everyone was afraid.

Then the Johnnies started rounding up the young men for a new Confederate Army. My two sons, George and Jesse, reached manhood as the war started. To me they were still boys. But the Johnnies came and got'em. My sons went along with them, declaring themselves Rebels. I was furious.

Jim had taught our boys how to be warriors. As they were growing up, he took them on hunting trips. At night around the campfire, he would tell them stories of the old days, of proud warriors and glorious battles. I guess our sons figured being Confederate soldiers meant they were warriors.

I argued with my sons. I told them, "Go west, hide out, do anything you can to avoid that war."

They laughed at me, told me I was "old-fashioned" and "too Indian."

George had grown so tall. He towered over me, saying,

"We don't want to stay here hiding in the woods, we want to go into the world. You want to be Indian, we want to be white."

His words burned into my heart like a dagger. I still feel the pain of those words. When they left to go with the Johnnies, they didn't even say goodbye.

I kicked the beautiful wooden bowl that Jesse had carved as a gift to my husband. I kicked it so hard, it split in two. Jim yelled at me, saying our sons really didn't have a choice. "If you are a male and of age," he shouted, "You are either a rebel soldier or dead. If you refuse to join the Confederacy, they call you a 'traitor' and kill you."

Then George, my first born who wanted so bad to go into the world, was killed in the Battle of Gettysburg.

Note from Ned:

As Annie spoke about her son's death, she stopped. Anguish covered her face; she looked at me. "You were with me when we found out," she whispered. "Say something!"

I told her my memories — Annie arguing with George and Jesse about the war. Her sons laughing at her. They told me that going to war would be a great adventure. And off they went. It was 1862.

In 1863, the Confederacy suffered a big defeat at the Battle of Gettysburg. The Alabama Battalion lost hundreds of soldiers. Preacher Jones told me that the Confederacy had posted the names of the dead in Market Town. I told my Aunt Annie and Uncle Jim about the list. Uncle Jim was sick, and couldn't walk those hours to Market Town. Aunt Annie stood up saying she was ready to walk right then. But she couldn't read the names.

Next day, Annie, Spring and I went to Preacher Jones. He wrote "George Hill" and "Jesse Hill" on a piece of paper. Annie said to the preacher, "My boys names are not 'Hill,' just George and Jesse."

The preacher told my aunt that soldiers had to have a last name, and her sons had chosen "Hill." Which makes sense since we live in the hills. The preacher gave me the paper with George and Jesse's names written on it, and told me that I should go with Annie and Spring.

All the way to Market town, my aunt kept saying to herself, "George is OK, Jesse is OK. They are healthy, they are strong." Spring didn't say anything, but I could see the fear in her big brown eyes.

When we finally got to Market Town, we saw crowds of people. Long sheets of white paper were nailed to the walls of a building. People looked intently at those lists. Some stood under the shade of the trees, weeping and hugging each other. Others looked relieved, and smiled. I started looking at those long lists of names. Holding Spring's hand, Annie stood behind me, whispering "No, no, no."

Then I found the name. "There," I said pointing, "George Hill."

"No!" shrieked Annie and Spring, bursting into tears.

I pointed to the name, and held up the paper Preacher Jones gave me with George's name on it. My preacher had told me that looking at the lists for my aunt was a big responsibility. If Annie's sons' names were listed as dead, and I didn't see them, it would be terrible for her to think they were alive, and find out later that they had died at Gettysburg. So I focused on doing my job. And when I found George's name, I felt proud of myself!

Remembering that day—over two decades ago—I felt terrible. George was a big brother to me. How could I feel proud of myself for finding George's name on the list of the dead?

I looked at Aunt Annie, now an old woman sitting in her

rocking chair under her oak tree. Her sad brown eyes looked back at me. "Oh, Auntie Annie, I'm so sorry," I cried, tears running down my face.

She stood up and hugged me, and we stood there holding each other and weeping.

"Ned, you were just a lad of fourteen," she whispered to me. "How brave you were to come with me that day. Keep telling me your memories. It's important to me."

So I continued to talk. Down there in Market Town on that sad, sad day, I looked at all the names on those lists again to see if my cousin, Jesse, was on that list. No, Jesse was not on the list. I found Annie and Spring sitting on the ground, hugging each other and staring into space. George was dead. And I still had a job to do, helping my aunt and cousin to get safely home.

That was so many years ago, but the grief of that day is still right here. Sitting in front of Annie's house, I felt overcome by sadness. Annie stopped the story-telling for that day.

I told my aunt that I needed to go back home to my family for a few days. At home, the sadness continued to drag me down. Talking to my wife helped, and so did going to church on Sunday. On Monday, I felt a little better, so I went back to Annie's house, and I read to Annie what I had written down. Then we picked up where we left off.

Annie continued:

What would I have done without my Ned? He is my nephew who is like a son.

When Ned showed me George's name, I stood there in a daze looking at that list. Then other people came to look for names of their loved ones. I moved away, sat down, holding onto Spring for dear life. Everything, everybody seemed far away. I felt numb. My little baby George, who grew into my big strong son, he couldn't be... no, no, he couldn't be dead. I looked around the crowd of people, realizing I knew no one there. Only Ned, and where was he?

Ned finally came back to us. "Jessie's name is not on the lists," he said. I didn't know what he was talking about. Later I realized he was telling me I had one son still alive.

Ned and Spring helped me get up, and silently I followed them home. I kept shaking my head. It couldn't be: George couldn't be dead.

Jesse, my dear sweet younger son, survived Gettysburg. And he survived other battles, as well as the diseases that killed so many soldiers. Jesse came home to us. But the war changed him. He came home a shadow. He told us he did not want to be an Indian. He yelled at us, and left home to go west. We never saw our son again.

Some months later, my cousin Tom, paid us a sad visit. (During the Indian Removal, he had moved to Oklahoma with his wife and her family.) Tom told us that after the Civil War ended, Jesse came out to Oklahoma, and stayed with them.

"Jesse was so restless. He was like a fire cracker looking for a match," Tom said. Just weeks later, Jesse got into a barroom brawl. The next day, Tom went to the bar to get Jesse. A man who worked there told Tom that white men had picked a fight, saying that Jesse "looked Indian," and that he shouldn't be in the bar, because "Indians can't hold their liquor." The insults led to a fight, and they beat Jesse bad. Then those men disappeared into the night. Cousin Tom tried to nurse Jesse back to health, but he was hurt too bad. Those men killed my Jesse.

Tom gave us Jesse's boots. We buried those boots in

our village burial grounds, along with some clothing he and George left in our house when they went to war.

Our two beautiful boys, gone. Eaten by that war. It sent my husband to an early grave. Jim was never the same after our sons died. He felt it was his fault that our boys joined the Confederates. I told him what he'd told me years earlier — that our sons didn't have a choice. But Jim was so sad, he pulled back into himself. Spring and I sang songs to him, because I knew we knew he loved our singing. But he lost the will to live. He faded away and died that winter. I wish I could have helped him more. I fed him, kept our house warm. But he had a sickness of the spirit, and no one could reach him. People said my husband died so he could join our boys in the spirit world. Might be true. Who can say?

Hiding out in Freedom Hills

The Civil War went on and on. There are so many sad stories, but also some good ones.

People call this area "Freedom Hills," because Indians, including us, hid here from the removal. Later, young men hid here to avoid the Civil War. My nephew, Will, was one of them. In his early twenties when the war started, Will was prime soldier age. Will persuaded his cousin Ben, Daisy's older son, to hide out with him. Will and Ben "disappeared" for over four years.

Will found a cave deep in the ridge where they slept, and told none of us where it was. Only his kid brother, Ned, knew where Will and Ben stayed. Ned was only twelve when the war started, and he was small for his age. But Ned, too, was cautious, staying away from the public as much as he could.

Will worked out a system of whistles to communicate with us. One whistle meant, "Take notice;" two meant "head for cover." Will and Ben had certain whistles to communicate with Ned. Our village always had a bunch of dogs. Will and Ned, following in their father's footsteps, knew how to train dogs. They taught them to roam at night, to seek out any strange people in our area, and howl if they found someone.

One night we heard the dogs howl. I watched Ned quietly leave the house next door. After a while, Ned reappeared, and tapped at my door. He told me Will needed me. Ned said I should come with him, bringing food and water. Ned had thrown several blankets over his shoulder. On our way there, Ned whispered to me that the dogs had found three people, white people. Will wanted me to help figure out what to do.

We walked down the steep rocky path away from our village. I was thankful that through the years, we had kept this trail hidden. The narrow path ended in the low meadow. After we walked a ways further, I saw three people standing with Will in the darkness, a man, a woman and a skinny boy. They were poor, white, and very dirty. Never in my life had I seen people so thin. Never saw anyone gobble down my corn meal mush so fast. Ned gave them blankets, and the woman and the boy laid down on the ground, but she kept watching us.

Will asked the man questions, and I listened. His name was Calvin Logan, and he had been a Confederate soldier. He deserted the army after he received a letter from his wife, telling him that she was pregnant, and that her mother had just died. She and their son were starving. Risking his life, Calvin deserted the army and got home to her. They fled, heading north, fearing any minute the Johnnies would find them.

As we talked, Calvin kept looking at his wife, lying on the ground. Ned gave him a blanket, and he curled up next to his wife and boy. Will, Ned and I moved out of voice distance from them. In Chickasaw, we discussed what to do.

Will said, "We've got to keep them away from the village."

I answered, "We have to help them, or they will die."

Ned agreed, saying, "It is the Christian thing to do."

Not wanting the church to have the last word, I added, "It's the Indian thing to do, too. I can't say about other folks..."

Will said, "Wait. First we need to think about the safety of our village. That is my main job. What if these two are spies?"

I scoffed, saying, "Spies aren't starving like that. Spies aren't pregnant and alone in the wilderness. We need Sissy to help this girl."

Will whispered, "What if the Johnnies come after her husband?"

I paused, "That is a good point."

Will thought a while, and then said: "We will help them. We will *not* take them to the village. They will stay here for the night. I will stay close by with the dogs. Tomorrow, Annie, you will send Spring to get Sissy to come to help. The boys and I will look around for a good place to build a shelter for them, downhill and away from our path to the village. "

We carried out Will's plan. Next day, Spring went to Sissy's house and brought her to see Nellie Jean. Appalled at the young woman's condition, Sissy decided to bring the pregnant woman to her home to care for her. Spring and I went along with Sissy, hoping we could help out. Nellie Jean miscarried the baby that night. Sissy nursed her through it all, and Spring and I cooked and cleaned and did whatever Sissy asked us. A few days later, Nellie Jean began to recover.

"God be praised," Nellie Jean said, her voice hardly a whisper. "Y'all saved my life!" Then she added, "I 'spected the baby wasn't gonna make it. But when we was out there lost in the woods, I feared I was gonna die, too."

Our spirits lifted as Nellie Jean got better. Spring, Nellie Jean, and I slept in what Sissy called the "living room." I had never been in a white home before. The house looked so big from the outside, but with Sissy, her husband, their children, and the three of us, the house was busy as a bee-hive.

Will, Ned and Calvin arrived and told us they'd found a good secluded spot and built a small shelter for the Logans. Will said it was good for our village to have a family living there, because that southern slope was the most vulnerable part of our hidden village. If they found our hidden trail, men on horseback could ride right up into our village.

That is how three frightened white people came to be our neighbors and friends. They loved us, we had saved their lives. After the war was over they built themselves a home in the lower meadow, on the southern slope of our village. We became close friends. Gus, their little skin-and-bones child, grew strong and tall. Nellie Jean got pregnant again, and had a healthy baby girl, they named Susie Mae. Gus and Susie Mae became good friends with our young folks. We had no idea back then how close we'd all get, and how much they would help us in the years to come.

Saving Nellie Jean's life meant a lot to me. It felt good to be able to help. It got me out of my lonely hurting.

Those war years were hard, starving times. The men, except the old ones, were forced to fight in that war. They left their farms, and their women and children behind. Many white women didn't know how to farm, because the white men said, "farming is men's work" and "women are too weak to farm." So the men went to fight the war, and left their women and kids to starve.

At least we Indian women could grow food to feed our families. Every day, Eve, Spring, and I worked in the field with other women in our village. We traded vegetables with our white neighbors. We also gave crops to the church to give to women who had lost their husbands and had little ones to feed.

Nathan Bedford Forrest, Confederate General

Note from Ned Ridge:

Aunt Annie asked me to add another civil war story. It was about the time my father and Preacher Jones ran into the Union cavalry, and then a few days later, the Confederate cavalry.

After the war broke out and my big brother, Will, went into hiding, our village faced a big problem. Will had become our village chief just a year before war broke out. More than ever, our village needed someone who could travel to learn about threats against us. All of our young men had gone to war or were hiding. So the village elders selected Stephen, my daddy, a fifty-year-old man, to be our chief as long as the war lasted. Stephen spoke good English, and read a bit of it. And his good friend, Preacher Jones, was a white man. The preacher had a horse and wagon, and he visited the sick and needy far and wide. Dad started traveling with Preacher Jones, and it was a good way to find out how people in these hills were doing, including other hidden Indians.

For several years after the war began, the main problem around here was the Confederate Army's Home Guard, or Johnnies. They would track down and kill men who had refused to join the army, or who had deserted. Which was why Will and Ben had to hide out. The Johnnies killed a lot of folks, and burned down a bunch of homes.

But as far as battles, it was quiet around here. That is, until 1863, the turning point in the war, when the Union got the upper hand. That was when Yankee troops started invading Alabama. Over three years, the Union Army invaded northwest Alabama three times.

As luck would have it, my Dad and Preacher Jones crossed paths with the Union Cavalry in 1863. They were traveling eastward to visit Preacher Jones' cousin Betsy, whose husband had just been killed in the war. They traveled on Preacher Jones' horse and wagon with a load of food and clothing for the widow and her children.

All morning it was quiet, until they stopped to water the horse and take a break. It was at a crossroads, right next to a creek. They heard noise from the north. Quickly it got louder, and seemed to be headed in their direction. Suddenly, hundreds of Bluecoats came riding down the road. Most were riding on mules! (Confederates, they later learned, called them the "Yankee Jackass Cavalry.") Suddenly Dad and the preacher were surrounded by a group of mounted soldiers, guns drawn and pointed at them. The soldiers took the preacher's horse, wagon, food, and even their hunting knives. Meanwhile, the cavalry kept passing by, as Dad and the Preacher stood there, now with nothing but the clothes on their backs.

Even without his horse and wagonload of food, Preacher Jones was determined to get to his cousin's house. As they walked the rest of the way, the preacher mumbled, "There's no such thing as 'good guys,' when an army marches through. No matter which side they are fighting for, or which side you're rooting for, they will take everything from you."

When they got to his cousin's farm, they were hungry. And they had nothing to offer the grieving family. Fortunately, neighbors had given the widow some food, and she cooked them supper. They stayed to visit, and spent days helping her to lay in food for the winter.

Dad and the preacher's adventure was not yet over. As they walked home, they came to the same crossroads where they had been robbed by Union troops. Again they heard the sound of horses coming from the north, heading towards them. This time they quickly hid in a thicket of bushes away from the creek. This time it was the Confederate Army from Tennessee riding south, in hot pursuit of the" Yankee Jackass Cavalry."

A big ferocious-looking man, on a huge horse, led the troops. It was Nathan Bedford Forrest, always called Bedford Forrest. General Forrest ordered his troops to stop and water their horses. Everyone dismounted and milled around while the horses drank. Then the General cracked his whip and swung back onto his horse. In a wink, all the soldiers were back on their horses in formation to ride.

"Where's that pickaninnie with my drink?" bellowed Bedford Forrest.

A small black child, dressed in rags, ran up to the General, holding up a flask. As Bedford Forrest grabbed the flask, the boy turned to run back where he came from. The General cracked his whip, flicking the child and drawing blood on the boy's little legs.

Silently the child disappeared into a wagon. And the mounted brigade quickly moved down the road.

Still hidden in the bushes, my dad looked at the preacher, whispering, "That was cruel!"

"We're lucky to be alive," mumbled Preacher Jones.

Bedford Forrest was infamous for his cruelty. Late in the war, his forces murdered hundreds of Union prisoners of war. A year after the Civil War ended, Bedford Forrest became the Grand Wizard of the Ku Klux Klan.

8.

Murder by "Parties Unknown"

When the war ended, we were so relieved. No more Johnnies. No more slavery. No more violence. We thought better times awaited us. But it was a sad, sad time for me. My house used to be so full. Now my sons and my Jim—all gone from this life. My world had shattered, and I didn't know how to pick up the pieces. Only one little girl left. Thank goodness I had my Spring.

Before the war, Market Town was safe. But when the Civil War began, Confederate soldiers came to Market Town with guns drawn, and took all the crops away from the farmers. After that, there were no more farmers' markets. People stuck close to home. When the war ended, many farms lay in ruins. But Mother Earth is generous, and crops started growing again. Farmers who grew more than they needed once again came to the Saturday farmers' market. Little did I imagine the suffering this market would bring.

During the war years, Spring became a woman, a beautiful young woman. Her light-brown skin contrasted with her dark eyes and her long braids of glossy dark brown hair.

When the war was over, Spring and her cousins began going back to the market. They saw friends they hadn't seen for years, and made new ones as well. Sometimes there were barn dances after the market closed. Spring learned how to "clog," a dance popular among the white country folks. Someone gave Spring a pair of clogging shoes. One day Spring showed me how she could dance. She put a flat wooden board on the ground, and she clogged, stomping her feet, faster and faster, holding her skirt so it swished with the beat. Such a racket! It hurt my ears. But what a smile on my daughter's face.

Spring met someone she fancied in Market Town. I suspected she was pregnant because she didn't go to her moon lodge. When she missed the second moon, I asked her, "Are you carrying a baby?"

Spring lifted her head proudly, smiled, and didn't answer me. I let the matter drop. Spring was a woman, and it was not my way to pry. By the third moon, I asked her again. This time Spring told me she was pregnant and happy about it. She told me not to worry.

Of course, I worried. The year before, Jenny had died in childbirth. Jenny was Spring's age, young and strong, the daughter of my cousin Wilma. Spring and Jenny grew up together, and shared the Moon Lodge when they were on their moon.

Spring never told me about her baby's father. When I asked, she shrugged and said, "He's nice." She never told me his name or anything about him, only that she was happy to be carrying a child. And in due time, Spring gave birth to Willow, a healthy baby girl.

Baby Willow's first summer was a good one. Our farm did well, and Spring went to the market with her cousins, carrying her baby on her back. She told me her friends there were happy to see the little one, and that she couldn't wait for Willow to get bigger so she could take her to a barn dance.

It was such a relief for the war to be over, and to have Will and Ben out of hiding, moving around freely. Stephen gladly stepped down as Chief, and his son, Will, once again became our chief, visiting the pockets of people who had refused to remove to Oklahoma. Families like ours were still living here in our homeland, even if some white people said we were "illegal."

Will came home from his travels with terrible stories about Negro people being attacked, even killed. The Confederates had lost the war, but they still said, "The south is white man's country." Just a year after the war ended, former Confederate soldiers built the Ku Klux Klan, with Bedford Forrest as the leader. They were nightriders who dressed like ghosts in white robes, burned down homes, and killed people. They wanted to return to the "good 'ole days of slavery."

Just a few moons after Spring's baby was born, over a hundred Klansmen marched through Florence, a city not far north of our village, and killed four people. It was 1870, right before state elections, and white men, with hoods covering their faces, murdered freemen for trying to vote. And another group of so-called "good 'ole boys" killed northern white teachers who were teaching colored people to read.

The KKK scares me, because they see us Indians as "colored." I said we all should stay close to home, and not go to the farmers market for a time. But our young people said that our village needed to sell our crops so we could get through the winter.

I spoke to Spring about my fears. She said, "I have to go to Market Town." I saw that determined look in her eyes. She was hardheaded, just like my mother.

We had four young folks in our village, and they said they would travel as a group to Market Town and stick together. Three strong young men-Will, Ned, and Daisy's son Ben—would look out for Spring. No one in our village thought people would dare attack folks here in the hill country where so many people hated the Confederacy.

On Market Day in the middle of that summer, Spring and her three cousins left at dawn. She gave me little Willow, telling me, "I will be back before dark." Those were the last words I ever heard my daughter say.

Spring was intent on going to the market that day. When she and her cousins left, I felt my stomach clutch, but it did not last. Life was all around me. Little Willow toddled around, and I followed her. She kept me busy all day. We had fun in the garden where I told her the names of all the plants. And we ate lots of grapes, until our fingers and mouths turned blue.

Suddenly a hawk shrieked. I saw the bird circling high overhead, and my heartbeat quickened. Willow looked up, but quickly returned to digging in the garden. I glanced around. Everything in the village seemed peaceful. I went back to tending my granddaughter.

As the evening sky darkened, a feeling of dread came over me. Little Willow would not fall asleep. Holding her in my arms, I paced outside my house. Darkness fell. Clouds blocked the moon's light. At long last, my granddaughter fell asleep, and I took her home to bed.

A sharp cry of mourning woke me up. Something terrible had happened! It was the dead of the night. Our three young men ran up to my home, and stood there panting. They looked at the ground, not looking me in the eye. I saw Will's face and dropped to my knees. Ned burst into tears. Eve stooped and took the baby from my arms. Will finally spoke, "Spring is still alive. Come with us now."

"No, no, no," I cried, burying my head in my arms and hiding my face in the grass. Friends from the village gathered 'round. Daisy handed me my cloak and my walking stick. Eve handed me a bag with cornbread and a flask of water.

Will and I left the village, walking rapidly. Several times we stopped to drink and eat. Will wanted me to rest, but I could not. I needed to get to my daughter.

As we entered Market Town, the pre-dawn light began filling the sky. My nephew led me to the colored side of town to a house, where a dim lantern flickered in the window.

An African woman met us at the door. "I'm Berta," she said as she led me to the bed in the middle of the room. "I'm so sorry." Spring lay there, breathing but unconscious.

"Those Confederates, those bullies who call themselves the Ku Klux Klan, they tore her up bad," whispered Berta. "In her woman parts. I've been trying to stem the bleeding, but she's lost a lot of blood."

Berta pulled up a chair next to the bed and I sat down, putting my head on Spring's bed. Exhausted, I fell into a deep sleep.

A hand touched my shoulder, and I woke with a start – where was I? Too quickly it came back, and tears ran down my face. I looked at my daughter, still breathing, still holding on. Berta handed me a bowl of soup, and sat down next to me.

I cried. "My daughter was at the market selling vegetables, her three male kin with her. The market was full of people. I've heard about the Ku Klux Klan as nightriders. But this was full daylight! Why didn't anyone do anything to stop those men?"

"It's so evil," whispered Berta. "When a group of white men decide to rape our women, often there's nothing our folks can do. The whites have the guns, the laws, and the courts.

"The Ku Klux Klan is just a new gimmick for an old crime," Berta continued, wiping tears from her eyes. "This kind of rape has long been happening on slavery plantations. Now, we are supposed to be free, but it gets worse. They just take some pretty young girl off the field with everybody looking on. They take her out of sight and have their way with her. They want to make us afraid. They are the bosses. Our lives, our children's lives, are worth nothing to them."

Berta then left me alone with my daughter. I talked to Spring, held her hand, sang every song, and prayed every prayer I knew. Slowly, slowly, she slipped away into the spirit world.

The world closed in on me. I went numb, everything blurred. Thank goodness for the steady presence of Berta. So calm, so strong.

Berta allowed me to just sit, staring into space, sometimes dozing. In the morning, she gently led me to her back yard, and sat me down on a chair that faced her herb garden. How could this mid-summer day be so beautiful with Spring dead? I smelled mint and sage, and the sun felt warm. I dozed.

Hushed voices came from inside Berta's house. I turned my head, and saw shadowy figures through the curtains talking to Berta. I dozed again. The sun was low in the sky when I awoke to Berta's soft touch.

"Who were those people?" I asked Berta as I followed her into the house.

"Concerned folks," she answered. "Nothing you need to bother with."

"I want to know," I said.

"No you don't."

"Yes, I do!"

"Well then," Berta paused. "It was the sheriff."

"The sheriff!" I said, suddenly alert.

"This may be too much," Berta sighed.

"I want to know," I growled, struggling to speak. I looked at Berta for a sign of hope. But there was precious little in the way of hope in her sorrowful brown eyes.

"Okay, but it's real bad. The sheriff heard Spring had passed. He came to 'vestigate. I asked him about murder charges."

Berta paused and looked at me. "He said 'no charges' for murder or anything else! He said Spring was killed by 'parties unknown.' "

"'Parties unknown?' What's that?" I asked. To me a "party" meant a get together to celebrate the harvest, or some other happy event.

"A 'party to a crime' is a person who commits a crime," explained Berta. "'Parties unknown' means they don't know who committed the crime."

"But people saw those men attack Spring and drag her off."

"That's true," said Berta. "The ones that did it *are known*. But 'round here, what 'parties unknown' *really* means is white men dragged off a poor colored girl. Yes, those men committed murder. But they are white–they get away with it."

I sat there in stunned silence, anger welling up inside me. "In my Indian tradition," I muttered, "when a person murders another, the family avenges the death by killing the murderer. A life for a life-that is justice to us. And these white people call *us* savages. There's *no* justice in the white man's way. Whites get away with murder."

"You got *that* right," Berta responded softly. We sat there in silence. Berta pointed to a couch. I lay down, and must have dozed off. It was dark when Berta woke me. 'Will's here to see you," she whispered.

Will came and put his arms around me, wailing into my shoulder. He whispered, "We need to bring Spring home for burial. The Logan family is sending their boy, Gus, with the horse-drawn wagon to bring her home. Do you want to walk back with me tonight? Or wait until tomorrow night and come home in the wagon?"

"I will come with Spring tomorrow," I mumbled, "If that is all right with Berta."

"Good," replied Berta. 'We have much to do to ready the body. Annie, I would like your help."

The next day, Berta and I bathed Spring's body with lye and goat soap, and rinsed it with Berta's powerful mixture of mint and rosehips and other herbs. Berta sewed a burial dress out of white muslin.

I watched Berta, wondered about her story. "How can you survive as an African woman in this hateful town?" I asked

"It ain't easy to live with cruelty all 'round," Berta said.

"But I'm lucky. I learned useful skills, and made friends with folks who need my help. 'Specially the women. I know just about everyone in this town, even those violent men. I know their wives, and birthed their children.

"I came up learning the ways of herbs," Berta continued, "and how to care for the people." Berta told me about her grandmother, a medicine woman in Africa. Along with many others, men forced her grandmother onto a slave ship headed to America. She brought her knowledge of medicine with her, and learned the ways of the herbs of this land. She used her knowledge to help the slave owners as well as the colored people. And she taught Berta, her granddaughter, everything she knew.

Berta did have a stroke of good luck. When her masters, in their old age, moved from their plantation to Market Town, they brought Berta with them. Berta took care of them. At his death, her slave master willed that Berta was "a free person," who would live in their house. She's lived there ever since. She planted an herb garden, and became a medicine woman for Market Town.

When she told me this, I reached over and held her hand and smiled at her, saying, "I'm glad you managed to stay alive and help so many people."

"In the last decade, I have delivered nearly every child born in this town," Berta responded, "Including that boy who loved Spring."

"What 'boy who loved Spring'?" I shouted, feeling anger well up inside me. "How could he 'love Spring'? Who is he? How could he let them attack her, rape her?"

Berta abruptly stopped sewing Spring's funeral dress. 'We'll make tea, and talk *quietly* in the garden."

I felt like a hand was gripping my neck, strangling me. I couldn't take my eyes off Berta as she prepared the tea. I watched a frown come over her face, as she struggled with herself over what to tell me.

My lips twisted in a knot, my eyes shut tight trying to hold back the tears, my arms were shaking as we walked out into the garden and sat down. Berta looked at me sadly, and whispered, "Say what you need to say."

"That boy got my Spring pregnant!" I cried. "He never came to our village, never even met me. And he let her get attacked and killed. What kind of 'love' is that?"

The blood pulsed in my head. I knew my voice was loud again.

"I'm talking softly, "said Berta. "If you need to yell, we'll to go inside and shut the windows."

"I will listen quietly to what you have to say," I said meekly.

"His name is Joe. I've known that young man since his birth." Lowering her voice, Berta looked directly in my eyes. "He's a good boy. I know he loved Spring."

Berta told me that Joe's mother died a few years back. After that, Joe's father took to drink, and started hanging out with violent men they call 'good 'ole boys.' Joe's father and his friends were furious that Joe had fallen in love "with a goddam Indian girl," and fathered her baby. The father demanded Joe stop his relationship with Spring. But Joe refused.

Then those "good 'ole boys" must have plotted the attack. One of them hired Joe to harvest his crops on that day, so that Joe would not be at the market when they attacked Spring.

"Joe came over here," Berta said, "as soon as he heard what happened to Spring. I never seen a man cry so bitterly. He told me he would not stay in this town any longer. He left that night, so I'm told, to go west."

"My poor Spring," I whispered, tears running down my face.

That night, Will and Gus arrived with the Logan's horse-drawn wagon. Berta and I gently wrapped Spring's body in a blanket, and the men placed her in the wagon. They gave me the choice of riding up on the bench with them, or in the wagon with Spring. I lay next to the body, even though I knew it was no longer my Spring that I was lying next to. Her spirit had left.

As I lay there, looking up at the clear night sky with all those stars, there were moments when I had no thoughts or feelings. But mostly I longed for the old days of my youth, when we could just be Chickasaw, and live according to our traditions, our ways. And I longed for the days of my marriage, mothering my children, hidden in the heart of Freedom Hills.

The clip clop of the horse lulled me to sleep. In a dream, my three children came to me, all alive, vigorous and beautiful. They were chasing each other around our village, laughing, playing. They waved to me. I saw love in their eyes as they ran off, disappearing into the field. I woke up and looked up at the stars. How can I live in this world without my children?

We got to the village at dawn. Gus and Will helped me out of the wagon, Will lifted me in his arms, and carried me up our hidden path to our village. Behind us, Ned and Gus carried Spring's body. They sat me in a chair facing east. I watched the sunrise, feeling nothing.

"I don't want to live," I mumbled to no one in particular. "I wish it was me you were gonna put down that hole."

But my family wouldn't let me go. They surrounded me with love and kept me busy with the serious matters at hand. People gathered. My whole village was there, and so was Sissy with her husband and young children. And there was the family we rescued during the Civil War–Calvin and Nellie Jean Logan, with their children, Gus, and little Susie Mae. Several Indians from other hidden places also came, and Will introduced me to them.

We sang the Mourning Song to a slow drumbeat. We walked in silence through our cornfield to our burial grounds. Our young men gently carried Spring's body, dressed in white muslin and wrapped in her favorite blanket. They lowered my daughter into her grave, right next to the rocks marking where we buried the remains of George and Jesse and Jim, nearby the graves of my parents, and all the others who had lived and died in our village.

People made a circle around the grave, and the drummers began the Blessing Song. Ned offered an old Chickasaw burial song. People sang, spoke, and drummed for Spring, for her short but courageous life. It was the drum that reached me, made me feel the beat of my own heart. My spirit lifted for a moment. Perhaps I was feeling Spring's spirit rising.

Then Calvin, Nellie Mae, and Gus lifted up their fiddles. They played a sad soft tune at first. Then they picked up the beat, getting faster and faster. I closed my eyes, and before me there was Spring dancing with her clogs, making a racket with those wooden-soled shoes. So alive, so beautiful.

For three moons after Spring's death, the whole village mourned. They hovered over me, never leaving me alone. Spring's cousins, aunts, uncles, and friends told me so many stories about her kindness, her spunk, her sense of humor. Truly, I was not alone in my pain.

I told my relatives what Berta told me about Joe, that

he did love Spring. Will and Ned recalled their memories about Joe, agreeing that he was a good man–not like his father and those violent men.

Our farmer neighbors brought food to me, and told us how sad they were about Spring. They were outraged that the town sheriff did nothing. People told me about other murders, where "parties unknown" meant no one was found responsible and no one was punished.

The days and moons blurred into each other, and the weather got colder. Sometimes I wanted to die. The mornings were 'specially hard. Spring and I had shared the same bed, and when I awoke and opened my eyes each morning, I still expected to see her lying there. When she wasn't, it made me wish the sun had not come up at all.

My granddaughter gave me the biggest reason to live. Eve cared for Willow while I was in Market Town, and when I got back, Willow had both of us as "mommies." Gradually I became her main mommy. She clung to me and Eve. Fortunately she had been weaned before Spring died, and ate solid foods with a hearty appetite. Toddling on wobbly little legs, she explored. I tried to keep up with her on my wobbly old grandmother legs. Will and Maya's children played with her, and we managed the best we could.

Eve was so helpful. My dear sister helped me from sinking into despair. She reminded me of the story my father told of the starving man and the wolves. An old man had lost his whole family, and he was starving. He traveled far out into the woods to the place of the wolves. He asked the wolves, "How can you go on living while white men want all of you dead?" And the wolves answered, "We just go on. We do today what we need to do to keep alive."

I've never seen a wolf. Would love to see one. They used to live around here, but the white men paid Indians to hunt the wolves 'til there were no more, sort of like the Indians. The same thing happened to the deer. Thankfully the deer are starting to come back. I love to watch them. Their lives are precarious. They are cautious, calm, alert, and graceful. I feel the deer's spirit. Like my village, they are just trying to survive and raise their young.

Following the way of the deer, I kept on doing what I needed to live. Eve and I prepared for winter, drying corn, preserving vegetables, gathering wood. Our relatives and neighbors were kind when the cold weather came, bringing us food and blankets and clothing for little Willow. And that was how we got through that sad winter.

Hard times set in the following year. Drought came in the summer, and scarce rain meant a poor crop. We preserved what we could, but that winter we were all very hungry. Our beloved Stephen, Eve's husband, caught a high fever and died all of a sudden. Willow and I moved into Eve's house to care for her in mourning. Lack of food haunted us. Willow cried, needing more than we could provide. Our relatives gave us what food they could, but everyone ran short. Our young people hunted squirrels and rabbits, and their precious meat kept us alive. Finally the weather began to warm up.

Then I had a nightmare about my granddaughter. In the dream, Willow had grown into a beautiful young woman, like her mother. And I watched powerless as white men raped and murdered her.

This nightmare got hold of me. I tried to put it out of my mind, but every time I closed my eyes, it was there. How do you protect your girl child if you can't protect yourself? Our three strong, young men couldn't protect

Spring. For weeks, my sister and I talked about that dream as we planted our spring crop.

After the summer solstice, I had another dream. In this dream, a good white man, a man with a family and a house, took in Willow as his own child. I felt that he would protect her. But did such a white man exist? And if he did, did he want a child, an orphan, whose mother was Indian?

My sister talked to her son, our Chief Will. And he thought on it. One day Will and the other men joined us to hoe a field. He told me and Eve, "Yes, I know of a man like the one in your dream."

Will said we would discuss the matter of my granddaughter in Chickasaw style in our Elder Council, in ceremony.

9.

The Decision

We gathered for the elder council – my sister Eve, my cousins, Daisy, Darryl, Wilma, and me. Will was in his forties, not yet an elder, but with the weight of the world on his back. He met with us because he is our village chief. After a starving winter, we needed to discuss our survival.

Our numbers had dwindled to only fifteen people in our village, down from twenty-four before the war. And more than half of those who died were the young adults. We were out of balance. We older folks might have had lots of wisdom, but our aches and pains limited our abilities to do what was needed to survive.

It was mid-summer, the Ripe Corn Moon. We met at sunset, a good time for ceremony, and made a sacred fire. We offered tobacco to the Creator, and smoked the pipe around the circle, and sang the blessing song.

Chief Will spoke, "Oh Creator, we are grateful for this land! Oh Mother Earth, we are thankful for the crops that grow in our fields, and our women's great skill as farmers. We are thankful for the squirrels and rabbits plentiful in our woods, and the men folks' hunting prowess that nourishes our children. We are grateful that once again there are deer in our forest. We thank you for the rains and the winds, and for the breath going in and out of our bodies. We thank you for all that you have given us."

Will paused deep in thought before he continued, "Ancestors! Today we ask you for your help. We ask with heavy hearts. How do we survive as a village? So many relatives have died, many of them too young. During the Civil War, we lost three of our strong young men: Annie's sons, George and Jesse, and Daisy's son John. When the war ended, we hoped for peace and the regeneration of our village. But then we lost Jenny in childbirth, and Spring to the people calling themselves a *clan*, the Ku Klux Klan.

"We come with heavy hearts today," Will continued, "to discuss the matter of Spring's daughter, our precious little Willow. Two dreams have come to our sister Annie. In one, Willow was attacked and violated, like her mother, despite our attempts to defend her. In the other dream, Sister Annie saw our dear Willow protected by a white family who took her in as their own child. We ask for guidance in this matter."

As Will talked, I wept. Ending his prayer, Chief Will looked at each of us, and asked, "How can our village survive?"

We talked about the deep hunger of the previous winter, and whether the crops we'd just planted would do better than the year before. With few strong young people among us, it was hard to do enough farming to feed us. Even if we had a good harvest, when the late summer crop came in, we could not count on taking it to market. The violence against the dark-skinned people made the market again dangerous.

We talked about each person in our village, the fifteen

of us. We still had three able-bodied young men, the ones who had tried to protect Spring. Some of them talked about going west, or north, to look for work. We did not want them to leave us, but we knew they would make up their own minds.

The situation facing our young people threatened our survival as a village. For us elders, our bones were weary, our joints achy. It was hard to work out in the summer sun, hard to work in the cold.

We sat quietly for a time. Then Chief Will spoke in detail about what he had learned in this travels about the Ku Klux Klan trying to make the Africans slaves again. These violent men sometimes attacked Indians, justifying their horrible deeds saying Indians were "illegal" and were flaunting the Indian Removal law. White men were forming secret Ku Klux Klan groups because they were angry, Will told us, and they blamed the colored people for everything. This was happening even here in the Freedom Hills among families that had been against the Confederacy.

Then Chief Will spoke about my dream of a white man's family taking in Willow as their own. Will said, "I know a white man who is good, whose family has been friends of the Chickasaws for generations. His name is Judge Jack Farrell. His father, Jesse Farrell, came to these parts long ago, and asked Chickasaws for permission to settle here. Jesse Farrell wanted Alabama and Mississippi to be places where Indians and whites shared the land in peace."

Will told us that Jesse Farrell was close friends with our late Chief Itawamba, and together they worked to keep our Chickasaw lands in Chickasaw hands. When the Jackson's Indian Removal came, Jesse Farrell stood with our people. While he lived, he lived as a Chickasaw, and when he died he was buried like a Chickasaw. "Jesse Farrell is part of us in life and in death," said Will.

Jesse Farrell's son, Jack, followed in his father's footsteps. He learned the medicine herbs from an old Chickasaw root doctor, and to this day practices Chickasaw medicine.

"Annie," said our Chief, looking at me, "you would *like* this man. He spoke out against the Confederacy, just as you did. Jack Farrell was a Unionist. The Confederate Johnnies told Judge Jack Farrell that they were going to recruit soldiers at his courthouse. Judge Jack said 'No!' When the Johnnies came, they saw the Union flag flying over that courthouse. And they saw Judge Farrell with 100 armed Unionists from these parts gathered below that flag. No one joined the Confederacy that day. And not a shot was fired."

Chief Will concluded, "This man could be a good protector for little Willow."

I wiped the tears from my eyes, and mumbled, "Yes, he could." And the elders nodded their heads slowly in agreement.

Then there was another voice. "Never give a child away." It was Wilma, my cousin. Of course Wilma would disagree! She and I were the same age, the daughters of two sisters, and we'd both lived our whole lives in this village. And we *never* seemed to agree. She made me angry. Here I was making the most difficult and painful decision of my life. And she was hell bent on making it worse.

Chief Will looked at Wilma, and asked, "Would you take baby Willow in? Feed her as one of you own?"

Wilma thought for a moment. Watching her, I thought of her daughter dying in childbirth, leaving Wilma with a newborn to raise. When Spring was killed, it meant that both Wilma and I had lost our daughters, and both of us had to raise grandbabies. I thought that would've brought us together. But we still seemed to disagree about everything.

Wilma frowned. "No," she said slowly. "Can't take Willow in. I'm all of a tucker by the end of the day as it is. It'd kick the stuffin' outta me to raise another young'un. Times is hard. Not enough food. Hope y'all understand..." Her voice trailed off, pinched maybe by the weight of guilt.

It was dark. An owl hooted in the distance. Will looked at Wilma, and then at me. For his whole life, he had watched us bicker. "We will sleep on this idea. Annie, tell me what you decide. Then I can go and talk to Judge Jack to see if his family is willing."

That night I watched my granddaughter as she slept. A wave of sadness washed over me. But then I felt a flicker of hope. Willow deserved to be safe and free. Why should she suffer? Her daddy was white, and she could pass for white easier than the rest of us. I slept soundly the rest of the night, and in the morning I asked our Chief to go and talk to Judge Jack.

During the Chestnut Moon, Will headed down the path to the Military Road he had traveled so often to keep up with family, friends, and acquaintances. On his travels, Will acted like a farmer, a white man in dress and in language. He always wore a hat to prevent his skin from turning too dark, fearing the whites might arrest him and send him to Oklahoma, "land of the red man." Will made lots of friends with white farming folks, who assumed he was white.

On this trip he planned to introduce himself to Judge Jack, to see if his family might adopt little Willow. After days journeying under the sun of the Chestnut Moon, Will returned and told us about his travels, especially the memorable afternoon he spent with Judge Jack.

"I found the Judge near his house, sitting on a bench in his sweet potato patch," Will said, describing Jack's home, which was also his courthouse. It was a big house, painted white, with big columns across the front

"Hallito! Chokma?" (Hello! How are you?) Will said.

Taking a corncob pipe out of his mouth, the Judge answered, "An Chokman." (I'm good.)

"Jack and I spoke in Chickasaw about our people," Will continued. "We found out that we are relatives."

"I knew you were an Indian," the Judge told Will, "even before you opened your mouth."

"How could you tell?" asked Will, "I'm trying to look like a white farmer."

"It's the way you move, "said Jack. "Quiet, like you are part of the woods. So different from white men, rich or poor, who swagger like they own the road."

"I grew up here when this was Chickasaw land," Jack told him. "My family's roots are in England and Virginia, but we moved here as guests of Chickasaw Chief Itawamba. His family shared everything they had with us, because we were respectful. But that was a long time ago. So much has changed."

Judge Jack took another puff and explained that the locals call his family "Indian lovers," and he was proud of that. Will and Jack covered a lot of ground that afternoon, sitting on the bench in the sweet potato patch. During the Civil War, Judge Jack defiantly flew the Union flag over his courthouse. But then the Confederates recruited Jack's son. His son died of fever in the army, as so many did. It broke Jack's heart, and he lowered the "stars and stripes." His union zeal was defeated by love for his son.

Will finally brought up the main reason for his visit to Judge Jack: Spring's death and little Willow. Jack had heard about the murder. His eyes widened as he looked at Will, and nodded as if to say it was no longer a casual conversation, and perhaps they were no longer on safe footing, even in his own garden. He leaned over and said quietly, but with anger on his tongue, hotter than a Mexican pepper. *"It's outrageous that the sheriff pulled that 'parties unknown' excuse."*

Will told Jack that Spring's death left a little baby girl motherless, and asked if Jack's family might take that child in as their own.

Will looked Jack straight in the eyes and held him in his gaze. In Chickasaw, Will said "Sho-ta-ha!" Then pressed his fist to his heart as a sign of respect, and again said "Sho-ta-ha!" (I'm all run out.)

"Jack sat like he was frozen in thought," said Will. "His silence felt like forever."

Then the Judge said, "I hear you cousin, I hear you my friend. Times are hard for all of us. My wife is sickly, and my daughter has her hands full raising her son. Don't know what they would think about bringing another child into the family. But I'll talk to them. Come by under the next moon and we will talk again."

As I sat listening to Will, so many emotions ran through me. Judge Jack talked Chickasaw. He was friendly. His family opposed the Removal and the Confederacy. And like me, Jack had lost a son to the war. I thought it was good that the Judge was going to discuss adopting Willow with his wife and daughter. So many of these white men just make all the decisions by themselves.

That summer I spent all my time with Willow. I spoke to her, and sang to her, in Chickasaw. We had fun in the garden, and grew a bumper-crop that year.

During the new moon in September, Chief Will met a second time with Judge Jack. He met Jack's wife and daughter, and ate a meal with them in the big house. Afterwards, Jack explained to Will, in private, that his wife was against bringing another child into their home, because she was sickly and a small child running around would be hard on her.

But Rose, Jack's daughter, wanted to meet little Willow. Rose's husband had been killed many years ago, and that tragedy had cut short her dream of raising a big family. Rose's son, her only child, was almost twelve years old, a good boy, but no longer a small child. Rose seemed to want another little one around.

Jack told Will, "It'll depends on how Rose and Willow get along. A visit in October will settle it."

A visit to determine Willow's destiny! Oh, the preparations we made. To travel safely, we needed to look like regular white folks. The whole village helped put together proper clothes for Will, Willow, and me. Our medicine man, who lived alone up on the ridge, treated me with an herbal rub of arnica, comfrey, and white willow to help my achy legs make that long walk. And he told me to drink nettle tea every morning.

My nephews built a little wheelbarrow that we could put Willow in when we got to the Military Road, because she was too big to carry, too small to walk all that way.

The day of our journey arrived. I woke before dawn – worried, hopeful, scared. Already missing my granddaughter. Maybe this is all a mistake, I thought. Maybe Wilma is right.

Then I remembered Spring dying in my arms. "Please let this visit go well," I prayed. "Please let Rose and Jack love baby Willow."

We walked down the hidden trail from our village to the path that led eastward towards the Military Road. It took a long time. My strong nephews carried Willow and dragged her wheelbarrow, and she cooed happily. She liked being carried in her cousins' arms.

By the time we got to the Military Road, I felt very tired. I looked down that long road that stretched forever towards Jack's house, a long ways south of Market Town. There were lots of folks on the road. Farmers in their wagons. A few horse-drawn carriages with fancy people in them. But mostly it was poor folks like us, carrying loads or pulling carts.

Willow didn't like riding in the wheelbarrow. She wanted to walk. This was dangerous, with all the people and animals sharing the road with us. So it was slow going, 'til Willow got tired, and we put her to sleep in the wheelbarrow.

We knew it would take us more than a full day to travel, so we planned to stop overnight at Berta's. I was happy to stay with Berta, so she could meet little Willow.

It was late that night when we finally got to Berta's house, and Berta got to hold the sleeping child. The next morning, they met each other face to face. Berta took Willow in her arms, and the baby laughed. We ate breakfast and got back on the Military Road. Little Willow decided she liked riding in the wheelbarrow. Many fellow travelers stopped to make faces at Willow, and tell her how adorable she looked riding in that contraption. I was the slow poke that day, because my knees and ankles ached so.

Finally Judge Jack's big house appeared through the trees. Fanciest house I'd ever seen. A woman in a long cotton dress and kitchen apron ran out of the house towards us. "I'm Rose," she said in a friendly voice, but paid us no mind. Tears ran down her face as she looked at my granddaughter sitting in the wheelbarrow.

Rose looked at me, asking permission with her eyes to pick up Willow. I nodded, and she gently scooped my granddaughter into her arms. I held my breath. Little Willow smiled and held out her arms to Rose. A moment later, Willow squirmed to get out of Rose's arms, and toddled over to me to hide behind my skirt. Clutching my hand, Willow and I followed Rose to the house.

Inside, Rose served us warm biscuits and fresh mint tea in dainty china teacups. It was the first time I held a cup more delicate than a mug. We sat around in chairs with padded seats. Do you believe it? They padded the chairs so their rumps wouldn't get sore.

I had never been in a house like that, but I couldn't take my eyes off my granddaughter. She sat on my lap for a while, then crawled down and went over to Rose. As Rose smiled, Willow climbed into her arms. It was love. But then Willow toddled back to me, and it became a back and forth game.

After a while, we all walked outside to see the garden and Jack's famous sweet potato patch. We had a picnic on the lawn. Willow loved being the center of attention.

After lunch, Rose took me to her bedroom that she would share with Willow. A nice room with a crib big enough for a growing child. Rose asked me to show her how I put Willow down for a nap. So I sat down in the rocking chair, and rocked my granddaughter, singing her favorite Chickasaw lullabies. When she fell asleep, I placed her in her new bed in her new bedroom with her new mother.

That's when I felt the loss. Earlier, when Willow met Rose, I felt so happy and relieved. But now I started wondering when I would ever hold Willow again.

I wanted to leave quickly, before my granddaughter woke up. She would cry if she saw me leave her with strangers. But it was painful – I had been there for her for her whole life! Rose and Judge Jack offered to put us up, but Will told him we were staying in Market Town.

As we were leaving, I spoke to Rose and Jack. "Giving up this child is the hardest thing I've ever done," I said looking at each of them. "It's for her survival. I'm proud of being Chickasaw, but I want you to raise Willow as your white child. It's too dangerous to be an Indian girl in these times."

They nodded. They understood.

We quickly gathered up our belongings, and as we began to leave, I stopped. "Can I come and visit my granddaughter?" I asked, "Perhaps twice a year, in the spring and in the fall?"

"Yes, of course!" said Rose, and her father nodded in agreement.

We left quickly, and then my tears began to fall. I suddenly felt exhausted. "Sho-ta-ha," I said to myself, "Sho-ta-ha."

10.

Breathing

No daughter to talk to, no granddaughter to run after. What had I done? How could I give away my Willow?

Feeling numb, I sat all day, seeing nothing. I didn't farm or cook. If my sister and my village hadn't taken care of me, I would've disappeared.

But then Eve started getting on me. "You can't just sit there," she said. "You'll turn to stone." I felt like stone. When I got up, I felt stiff. Eve hounded me, "You're getting rheumatism! You gotta move around."

I closed my eyes, ignored her. Days passed, I slept, I sat, slept, sat. Then, one day, I saw the Rocky Ridge there in front of me. That ridge has always been there, rising up beyond our village's fields. But this was the first time in many moons that I had *seen* it. I closed my eyes, trying to ignore it. But the ridge was calling me.

White folks around here are always talking about "the devil." They call our ridges "the devil's backbone." They think our ridges are cursed. But I don't believe in the devil. That's churchy talk. I believe that mountains are sacred places to pray to the Creator and seek visions. Our ridge is a step closer to heaven, not hell.

I struggled with myself to answer the call of our rocky ridge. With much effort, I got up and on my feet. In pain, I walked, slowly and stiffly through the village. For days, I walked, warming up my bones. "It's time to go to the Ridge," I told my relatives. People smiled, happy to see me moving again. They knew what I meant. Time to go back to the source, time for a spiritual renewal.

An old trail goes up from our village up to the ridge top, where you can see for a country mile above the tree-tops. I've climbed that path since I was a child. Back then, I bounded up the ridge like a rabbit, running far ahead of my mother. Now, I am old and slow, leaning on a walking stick that my husband made me before he died. I guess he knew I'd need it eventually. I sure do need it now.

It was a warm fall morning, and the woods burst with life. Three bullfrogs jumped into the creek as I walked by. Squirrels scurried, chipmunks scampered, birds called. An old doe limped by me, her big sad eyes meeting mine. We acknowledged each other. Then she limped over to eat grass, doing just what she needed to live.

I came to the shallow spot where we cross the creek on stones. But there had been much rain, and water covered the steppingstones. I stepped slowly, sticking my walking stick into the creek to help me balance on the rocks. On the last rock, I slipped. One knee landed on the stepping-stone, the other leg in the water. Got my skirt and moc-casins wet. I scraped my knee, and pulled my back out. Thank goodness I was next to the creek side, and could pull myself up onto dry land.

Sitting there in the sun, I looked up through the trees at the Rocky Ridge. Maybe there was a shred of truth to this devil thing. Maybe that devil was trying to trip me up! I sat in the warm sunlight for a spell, and the sun dried my skirt and moccasins. But it did nothing for my back, which had decided to quit on me just as I was trying so hard to find a reason *not* to quit!

After resting a while longer, I decided to pay the devil no mind. "I'm going to climb up that ridge, up to the spot where I used to go with my mother," I told myself. It is a sacred spot where my mama would talk to her ancestors. My mother, my father, my husband, my sons and my daughter had all passed on. I hoped – I needed – to talk to their spirits.

As I struggled up the steep parts of the trail towards that magic place, hunger and thirst greeted me. No longer numb, I found the small spring with clear water and sweet berries. It felt good to feel hungry and then nourished. I saw a cluster of small sassafras trees, and dug one up, washed the root in the spring, and chewed it. Its sweetness spread throughout my body. For the first time in many moons, it felt good to be alive.

Finally, I came to the rocky ledge, where I could see over the treetops. I remember being small, my mother clutching my hand tightly so I would not fall off the rocks. Years later, it was me holding on to her arm so she would not fall.

But that day I was a grandmother alone. I sat down on a rock, looking out over the forest. I had lived my whole life nestled here in these hills. It is so different today, when young people run off to places I have never heard of –fighting wars, looking for work, or trying to escape from this life.

When I was a girl and looked out from this magical spot, I saw forest so thick it hid the hills and valleys. But that day, I could see where the forest had been cleared for farms. I saw a barn, and fenced-in fields, and other fields beyond that. In the far distance, I could see that Military Road. I'd always hated the Military Road, built by Andrew Jackson, whose men hacked through our beautiful forest. But now I needed that Military road. It's the way I could visit my granddaughter.

I sat in this magical place where my relatives had found comfort in the past. All I could think was, "What have I done? I have no children left. How could I give up my precious grandchild?" I found the spot where my mother had talked to her ancestors. It is set back from the ledge, where the moss is thick. Lying on the moss, I curled into a ball and cried myself to sleep.

When I woke, the sun was low on the horizon. I felt the presence of my mother, sitting there with me, like we'd sat together so long ago. I felt her words: "You've done the best you can. You've given your granddaughter a chance to survive. Let yourself mourn. But keep on living – the village needs you."

Mama understood. Tears fell, and calm flowed over me. I felt better even though my back and knee hurt.

Before leaving, I gave thanks to the four directions. With the sun on my back, I faced east, looking out across the land that used to be all forest. I spoke to the spirit of the east, "Thank you place of the rising sun. Thank you for this year's bountiful harvest. Thank you for the white families that live in harmony with us as our neighbors."

Then I turned to the south, where I knew the Military Road wound its way towards Willow's new family. "Thank you, spirit of the south, for the warmth and growth that you have brought us this year. And, yes, thank you for that darn Military Road that will help me visit my granddaughter."

I turned westward, facing the sun low in the sky. "Thank you, sun, for your light and warmth each and every day. Thank you for the winds and rain that come from the west, bringing us precious water."

I faced the north, greeting the place of cold and mighty winds. "Thank you for your wisdom and for the lessons the winters have shared with us. Help us to work together to get through the cold season that is coming. Help me to take care of myself so I can help others."

Finally I looked up. "Thank you, Creator for everything." And then I slowly and carefully made my way down the ridge towards the warm fires of my village.

My body hurt after my visit to the ridge. Eve heard me groaning, and I told her about falling on the stones in the creek.

Sister Eve touched my back and legs saying, "You need willow!"

I turned around and said, "Do you think so? Do you think seeing Willow will heal me? Will you come with me to see her? "

Eve started to laugh, then covered her mouth. "I'm talking about white willow – for your aches! You need white willow so you can heal and see your granddaughter again. I can make a salve for you. It'll make you feel better. Then you can go and see your 'white' Willow."

That year the winter came early. Snow and ice storms descended on us, unusual around here. I moved in with my sister, sharing her house. My sadness returned. I spent days staring at the fire. Eve told the relatives that I was "good at tending the fire." Keeping the fire going is what kept me going. On the coldest nights, we slept with Will's family next door, so we could all sleep together, keeping warm around the fire.

Hunger lived with us. We had a better harvest than the year before, and the village shared everything we had. But it was a hard, long, cold winter.

I also got sick, and people thought I was headed to the spirit world. But my sister would not let me go. "You still got work to do here," she said to me over and over, as she forced me to drink warm sage broth. She told me to talk to the tiny Chickadees. "They are the spirit of our Aunt Oktosha Foshi. They love even the coldest days."

In truth, the Chickadees' cheerfulness annoyed me. But I did respect their ability to live in the cold. I put seeds outside our window, and they called, "Chickadee dee dee. Hi Sweetie." over and over. I sometimes swore they were saying, "Oktosha Foshi, Chickasaw dee dee." The chickadees, and perhaps my aunt's spirit as well, helped me survive the winter. I was weak but alive.

In the spring, I hoped to visit Willow, but I was too sickly. Will went on his travels, stopping at Berta's house in Market Town. "Berta's the best source of news," Will said on his return, "because she knows all the women, and keeps an eye out for what's happening." Talking with Berta, Will found out more about the doings at Judge Jack's place than if he visited there in person.

Will told me that my granddaughter had made it through the winter in good health. What a joy to hear that! Rose loved her and doted on her, and Willow responded with laughter and affection. Hearing this, I was relieved - and jealous of Rose, who had replaced me as Willow's loving mama.

I'd made the right decision, I kept telling myself. The winter just past could have killed us both. But the pining for my granddaughter lingered in me.

As spring turned into the hot summer, I did what I could on our farm, but I was too weak to do much. Age also sapped Eve's strength. We held a women's council to discuss how to get the farming done. In our tradition, we decided to shift the responsibility to those who could best do the work. Maya and Will had three children who were big enough to help farm. Maya took on the responsibility for the garden and fields that Eve and I had tended. Eve's kitchen garden went to Maya. Eve and I shared my kitchen garden. Eve and I helped in the fields, and gave advice, but Maya was in charge. I was thankful for our village's young women who could relieve me of that farming responsibility.

I gave myself a new spirit name. "Foyohompa." It means to breathe, to be alive. That's what I'm doing. Just trying to survive.

11.

Long Walk

After the fall harvest, finally I felt strong enough to walk to visit my granddaughter. Thanks to Eve's salve made out of white willow, my back and legs felt better. So much for that devil who tried to trip me up. Eve helped me spite that devil at his game – using good old Indian know-how.

It was a full year since I had given little Willow away.

Leaving at dawn, I felt glad that I still could walk for hours. All these people were on the Military Road, many more than last time. More horse-drawn wagons and carriages. More people on foot.

I walked past two young boys, with fishing poles over their shoulders and fish still dangling from the sticks. As I passed by, one of the fish got loose from the pole, falling into the dirt. The bigger boy grabbed the fish, and it looked like there might be a fight between the two boys right there on Military Road. People gathered around. A preacher man made the big boy give the fish back to the small boy. Then preacher said he had some words of wisdom for the young'uns, "Always take your fish off the stick before you walk home." Everyone laughed. I laughed, too, for the first time in a long time. The preacher had rendered justice *and* saved the boys' friendship as well.

All the goings on made the day go by quickly. I got to Berta's house by mid- afternoon. Berta introduced me to a young girl named Casey. She was an orphan, living with Berta. Since Berta had no children of her own, she took in Casey to help her, and to teach her the way of herbs. About ten winters old, Casey was darker that Berta, and a fast learner. We prepared a delicious dinner, and chatted for hours about growing medicine plants, and how to use them for different ailments. Casey made me nettle tea, and a salve to rub on my achy feet and back. A big help, because I was sore all over.

The next day, I managed to get to Judge Jack's place. I found Rose and Willow in the garden. Willow had grown so big since I'd seen her. She nearly came up to my waist. She looked strong and energetic, and chatted away in English. Rose introduced me as "Auntie Annie." Willow glanced at me before turning her attention back to her rag doll.

My heart sank. Does she remember me? Is she angry that I left her? A year is a long time when a child is young, I told myself. But then hiding behind Rose's skirt, she smiled at me. We all three played "Peek a boo, I see you."

We ate lunch, and Rose put Willow down for a nap. Rose and I talked, and she told me how much she loved her adopted child, and how well she was growing and learning to speak.

"Does she ever talk Chickasaw?" I asked.

"No, I don't believe so. Don't know the language, so if she says words in Chickasaw, I wouldn't recognize them."

Later that afternoon, when Judge Jack appeared, I asked him if he ever talked Chickasaw to Willow. "No," he said, "Haven't talked to anyone in the old way since Will and I spoke last year. It's sad, but I think the language has pretty much died out around here. People are afraid to reveal they are Indian."

I said my goodbyes and left their house. With tears in my eyes, I walked back to Berta's. Rose clearly cherished my grandchild, and Jack was a good protector. But my heart cried for my grandchild because I couldn't hug her every day. And she was losing our precious Chickasaw language.

By dusk I got back to Berta's place. Exhausted, I sat on Berta's couch, and I told Berta about my visit. I asked what she knew about Judge Jack's family.

"He's a good man, compared to most," Berta replied. "He learned Chickasaw healing from the old Chickasaw medicine man, just as I did. And we both practice that medicine, him with the men and me with the women. But Judge Jack has never paid much attention to me. It may be because I am a woman, or maybe because my family is African.

"You know," Berta added, "Judge Jack had slaves until the war freed them."

"What?" I suddenly sat up and looked at Berta. "Judge Jack had slaves?"

"Yes, he did. He owned a slave family that lived there for generations on his farm. Jack was a better master than most. He never sold anyone in that family. Keeping families together was a big deal for us during slavery. Many plantation owners sold children from mothers, husbands from wives. A terrible, terrible thing to destroy families like that."

I was stunned. The protector of my granddaughter had

owned people! "I didn't see any colored people down there," I said.

"There are very few Africans around here," Berta replied. "That's 'cause this is not a friendly area for free colored people. As you know too well, there's evil white men who still kill people and get away with it. Many black folks people headed north as soon as they got free, following the 'drinking gourd,' the Big Dipper."

I muttered something about Judge Jack. And Berta added gently, "Judge Jack is not perfect. But he is a good man, and he loves your granddaughter."

I slept soundly that night, and the next morning I headed home. As I walked, I thought about Berta. Such a good, honest, wise woman, able to work with different kinds of folks. Outside of relatives, she was the person I felt closest to. I realized *I needed to stay with Berta,* whenever I visited Willow. I needed to talk to her to be able to visit Jack's house.

For many years after that, I saw Willow every autumn. I always stayed with Berta. I got to know Casey, and watched in admiration as she learned to be a medicine woman. Each visit, Berta and Casey taught me more about plant spirit medicine.

For the first few visits, I felt like a shadow when I was at Judge Jack's farm. I talked to Willow in Chickasaw, hoping she would remember some of the words that she used to know. She showed no interest. She might've said something to Rose, because as I prepared to leave their house, Rose asked me not to speak Chickasaw around Willow. "It is best for her to only talk English," she told me sternly.

That stung! My granddaughter was alive, and healthy. But *Willow was no longer Chickasaw!* How could she live without talking our language, without knowing our traditions?

As the years went on, Willow grew, and she recognized me when I visited. She loved growing vegetables, and proudly showed me her garden. We talked about growing things, and I told her how to talk to plants. Each fall I brought her seeds that I saved from my garden that harvest. And the following fall, she would proudly show me the vegetables she had grown from those seeds. Plants became the special thing we shared. Yes, Willow loved Mother Earth. At least that part of our Chickasaw tradition had remained with her.

Willow always called me "Auntie Annie," but I wanted her to know that I was her grandmother. I wanted her to know about her mother. I talked about this to my sister, and Eve made a suggestion, "You need to tell Willow some stories."

As I walked down to visit that fall, I thought about the story I wanted to tell Willow.

"How old are you, Willow?" I asked her when I saw her.

"I'm nine years old," she replied proudly. "I'm big, and I got a big garden. Did you bring me some seeds?"

"Yup. I brought you bean seeds and pumpkin seeds, and a mint plant."

"I love mint," Willow said as we headed to her garden. After she showed me her crops, we planted the mint plant. Then we sat on a bench in the sunshine.

"Would you like me to tell you a story?"

"Yes!" said Willow, looking at me with those brown eyes, just like her mother's. "I love stories." She lay down on the bench, putting her head in my lap, and I put my arm on hers. It felt so good to hold her.

"Once upon a time," I began. "A sweet baby was born

in a beautiful village in the mountains. The baby's name was Sassafras, and she lived with her mother and grandmother, who both loved her very much. Then one day when she was still a baby, some bad men hurt Sassafras' mother. And her mama had to leave this earth and go up in the sky to the spirit world."

I looked down at Willow to see how she was taking all this. She lay very still in my lap with her eyes closed. Was she asleep? I decided to keep telling this sad story.

"The grandmother loved Sassafras so much, and she tried hard to be her mommy. But times were hard, and there wasn't enough food to eat. So the grandmother looked for another Mommy to look after her grandbaby. And she found Mama Red Bud and Grandpa Joe. And she gave little Sassafras to them. And Sassafras grew and grew up to be a big girl. And that is my story."

Willow's eyes opened, and she looked at me. "Is that story about me?"

"Yes," I said. "I am your grandmother, and I love you very much."

Willow's eyes closed again, and she went to sleep, snoring softly on my lap. I sat there in the warm sun, holding my grandchild and softly singing her Chickasaw lullabies. A gentle breeze tickled the leaves, and my hair. I felt at peace. I felt Spring's spirit with us, felt Spring kneeling down right there with us, putting her arms around Willow, gently hugging her.

Then Judge Jack appeared, breaking the spell. He told us supper was ready. We ate and talked about the weather, the crops, and their new baby donkey. After supper, it was getting dark, and Judge Jack gave me a ride to Berta's house in his horse-drawn wagon.

I told Berta the story I told Willow. "Hmmm," Berta

said. "I wonder if Willow will tell Mama Rose. That woman's scared of everything."

"Don't know," I said. I thought about it the next day as I walked home. Rose did seem fearful. I remembered years earlier, when she told me not to talk Chickasaw to Willow.

The following fall, as I walked to see my granddaughter, I wondered if Willow had told Rose about my story. I feared Rose would chastise me. Fortunately, Rose was friendly as ever, and said nothing about a story.

Again Willow and I went out to her garden, where we planted some seeds I brought her. As we finished up, Willow asked me, "Please tell me another story."

I told her about Chickadee and Bluejay, and how they built a village in the forest, high in the hills where only birds could go. A happy village away from wars. Again Willow said she liked the story. Then we had supper with Jack and Rose, and Jack drove me back to Berta's.

I got to take this opportunity to talk to Jack, I told myself. "Judge," I started, my voice shaking. "Does Willow know about my daughter? Does she know why I come and visit her?"

"I don't think so," said Jack. "Willow's never said anything to me or Rose."

I hesitated, then said softly, "I feel like she should know. Do you mind if I tell her some gentle stories?"

Jack kept his eyes on the horse, his mouth twisting. After what seemed like a long time, Jack said, "We are very protective of Willow. You asked us to raise her as our white child, and that is what we are doing."

After another silence, Jack continued, "There are Indian haters around here. One hater family lives right over there." And he pointed to a house, and I looked at it, as we rode by. "The man of that house hates Indians, and his sons beat up a kid at Willow's school, calling him a 'half breed.'"

Jack told me that he understood my desire to tell Willow about her Chickasaw heritage. We had pulled up in front of Berta's house, but he kept on talking. "I want you to know that Rose has been a nervous person ever since her husband was killed back in 1860. She wouldn't want you to tell Willow any stories about Chickasaws."

Finally Berta came out to see if anything was wrong. I thanked Jack, and followed Berta through her front door. Berta fixed tea, and we talked late into the night. She told me about violence against Africans and Indians in Market Town. She told me what roads and farms I should avoid.

Berta looked at me, seeing me in my misery. "Annie, I'm going to tell you a story. You must promise to keep it to yourself.

"When I feel scared and sad," Berta began, "I think about my hero, a woman named Harriet Tubman. I learned about her from my cousin who went north after the Civil War, and when he comes back to visit, he tells me more and more about her.

"She is about your age, Annie. Born a slave in a state north of here called Maryland. As a girl, she learned the woods and the streams around her. She knew which way to travel towards freedom. In her twenties, she escaped from her masters. But once up north, she kept thinking about those she left behind. She decided to go back there into those slavery lands where she grew up, to lead people to freedom. She went back there, time after time, risking death, over and over.

"They called her 'Moses.' She dressed in a man's suit, carried a gun. She only took people who promised to do everything she told them. The whites put a bounty on her head, but they never caught her. She always went in wintertime, when the nights are long, and white people stay in their houses. She could hear and see in the dark. She never lost a person."

Berta sighed, "When I feel down, I think about Harriet Tubman. And her spirit helps me I do what I can do here. I've done things that I know Harriet would be proud of."

I asked Berta to tell me those stories. "Can't," she said. "Not now, not here."

I kept visiting Willow every fall. I walked down that Military Road, and always stayed with Berta.

I told Willow stories of our village and our people. I believe she kept them secret because neither Mama Rose nor Judge Jack ever said anything. The last time I walked to Judge Jack's farm, Willow told me she had turned thirteen years old. That visit I told her the story of the Indian Removal. I didn't know that it would be my last long walk.

Willow told me she was glad that I was her grandmother. Jack's wife, Nancy, had been sickly ever since I met her. On that visit, Nancy was bedridden

"My Grandmother Nancy does not like me," Willow said. "Whenever I am near her, she always says, 'Run along, sister Daisy.' What she means is 'Child — get away from me.'"

"People get cranky when they get old and sick," I explained, remembering that from the beginning, Nancy had been against Willow coming into their household.

"Am I a 'half-breed'?" Willow asked me.

"Who said that?" I asked her.

"No one. But at school some of the mean kids call some of the other kids 'half breeds.'"

"You are a beautiful young girl," I told her. "No one is a 'half breed. We are all *full* human beings. All people are mixtures of their mother and father. I am a 'mixed blood' because my father was Cherokee and my mother was Chickasaw. And you are a mixture of Chickasaw and white."

That winter my achy joints got much worse. I got rheumatism real bad. The cold tightened up my ankles and knees, and I could hardly walk. When it warmed up in spring, I needed a cane to move around my village. There was no way I could walk all the way down to Judge Jack's place.

As the years went by, and Willow grew into adulthood, I hoped that somehow she would figure out a way to come up and see me. But she didn't come. I tried to imagine how Willow was growing, what she was thinking. She was the age when a young girl needs guidance from an elder. But gradually as the years passed, I no longer felt her spirit like I used to.

During those rheumatism years, I befriended some of the youth in our village. Before then, I'd avoided getting close to them, because they reminded me of the loss of my children. I also feared that maybe I brought bad luck, because my own children had all died.

I'd been watching a girl name Misty, who was just a year older than Willow. Misty's mother had died in childbirth, leaving Misty to be raised by her Grandmother Wilma, the cousin I didn't get along with. Wilma's comment that she "could never give up a child" still hurt all these years later.

Because Wilma and I don't get along, I was surprised when Misty asked me to help her take care of our village's chickens. My rheumatism meant I couldn't farm at all. Caring for chickens is easier on the joints. At first I did it out of duty, because I needed to do something to contribute to the village. But then I began to enjoy the chickens. They are such characters, foraging through our village, eating bugs, and grass, and grains. They stick together as they watch out for hawks and foxes and raccoons. They talk to each other, sometimes fussing, sometimes sweet – just like us humans. They fertilize our cornfields and gardens, give us delicious eggs, and provide us with meat.

I liked working with Misty. She taught me about chickens, and I taught her about plants.

"How do you talk to plants?" Misty asked me.

"I'll teach you what my mother had taught me," I told Misty. "If you watch plants and listen to them, the plants will tell you what they need. "

Out in our fields, I showed Misty how the corn and the beans and the squash work together. We call them the Three Sisters. We put corn kernels in a mound, and then plant six or eight bean seeds in a circle around the corn. Then we plant some squash seeds in a bigger circle around both the corn and beans. By watching and listening to these plants, we learned that they help each other, they like to be together. The corn grows tall towards the sky, the beans need something to grow on and love to wind up and up around the corn stalk. The squash have such big leaves, and they like to be shaded by the corn stalk. And the squash helps the corn, because its big leaves help keep the weeds from chocking the corn.

"If you watch carefully you can see for yourself that the Three Sisters like to be together," I told Misty, as we walked out into our fields. On the edge of the field, I showed her where we ran out of bean and squash seeds, so we planted just corn kernels. I pointed to the few lonely corn plants, growing by themselves. They looked smaller and weaker than the nearby corn plants that had beans climbing up them and squash surrounding them.

"Those corn really love those beans!" said Misty.

"Yes," I said, "Those beans are doing something to the soil that is good for the corn. And we farmers love the squash, because their big leaves help us to keep the weeds from taking over. We work together with the Three Sisters, and get a good crop to feed all of us."

We each use our gifts to contribute to the survival of our village. We each specialize in something that is useful to others. For example, Misty's mother, my cousin Wilma, hates to farm. But she sews clothes for all of us, and she mends our garments when we tear them. I am all thumbs with a needle and thread, so I try hard to be nice to Wilma. That way she will keep repairing these old clothes. She even keeps sewing up the old moccasins for me.

One day Misty said to me, "Auntie Annie, would you be my grandmother?"

"You already got Grandmother Wilma," I replied.

"I want two grandmothers," said Misty. "I got so many questions I want to ask you."

"Well," I said, "I'll have to talk with your Grandmother Wilma." Adoptions when a child has living relatives require consulting with those relatives. You can't adopt a child just because she is angry with her mother.

Misty, a teenager, wanting me as a grandmother—that made me feel good. But I was sure Wilma would be against this adoption. I hesitated going over to Wilma's house because we'd disagreed with each other on important decisions. I remembered the terrible winter night when

Wilma's daughter died in childbirth. The next day, I went over to her house to offer sympathy, and Wilma got mad at me! And I'd never forgiven Wilma for opposing giving Willow up for adoption. Since then, I hesitated to be alone with Wilma, glad she lived on the other side of the stream from me. But now I needed to talk to her about Misty's request.

To my surprise, Wilma thought it'd be a good idea for me to be Misty's second grandmother.

"She's young, needs advice," said Wilma. "Been a big job to raise her by my lonesome. You are smart, out-spoken. That'd be good for Misty."

"But sometimes I am wrong," I said, remembering Wilma's words about my granddaughter.

"I think you were right, I never should've given up Willow." The words just came out of my mouth. But it is true, those starving years were but a distant memory. And I missed Willow.

"Your Willow's alive. Well-off," said Wilma. "Nothing's worse than losing a daughter – you and I know that."

Wilma paused, then continued to talk. "Only thing harder is havin' to make that decision yourself. When I spoke 'gainst you that night, I spoke from my own loss. Mean for me to say those words. I'm sorry."

We talked a while longer, then parted saying, "Good night. See you tomorrow." Were Wilma and I friends? Maybe, I thought, especially if we only talk about Misty, our shared granddaughter.

12.

Colored (Ned's Story)

Note from Ned Ridge, Scribe:

The next morning, Annie said to me, "Ned, I've been thinking about you, about your story. Weren't you supposed to be the teacher at that school next to Preacher Jones' church? What happened? Why did you up and leave our village?"

I knew my aunt was going to ask me that. She needed to know why I left, why I hadn't explained myself. So I had prepared myself to tell her:

I thought I would always live in this village. As a young boy, I learned to read and write English to help us. I worked for Preacher Jones at the Two Trails Crossing Baptist Church for more than a decade.

When I turned twenty-one years old, in 1870, Preacher Jones counseled me. "Ned," he said, "You are a man now. You are very smart and good with children. I think you should become a teacher. This town is talking about building a school, and you should be the teacher."

I had always wanted to do something important with my life.

My father had gotten our village to learn to talk English. He befriended Preacher Jones, and he was our chief during the Civil War. These were important things – they helped us survive. And for decades my big brother, Will, has been our chief. The village looked to my family to do important things.

But in 1870, I couldn't hear Preacher Jones tell me what I should do. Just a few months earlier, evil white men had killed Spring. She was my favorite cousin, and I was with her when those men dragged her away. What they had done to her! I couldn't get it out of my mind. Why didn't someone stop them? Why didn't I stop them? Over and over I had nightmares about it. Even years later that memory would come to me every day. I couldn't think about being grown, couldn't think about anything.

I moped around, doing chores and errands. I kept my routine, going to church on Sunday, singing in the choir, and helping Preacher Jones teach children how to read.

It took years for the folks in Two Trails Crossing to build a one-room school house next to Preacher Jones' church. My Aunt Sissy told me her children were planning to go to the school, and she thought children from our village should go to there too.

After a long time, the preacher spoke to me again: "Ned, it's 1874. You are twenty-five years old. You need to think about your future. And we need a teacher for our new school that's opening up this fall."

I looked up to the trees. Preacher Jones grabbed my shoulder, raised his Biblical voice and cried, "Ned, you could be that teacher!"

"Okay," was all I said. Time to stop moping, I thought to myself.

Preacher told me I had to go to a teacher meeting in Birmingham, to sign up for the job at the Two Trails Crossing school. He told me he would write a recommendation for me to take down there, as soon as I chose a last name. I remembered that

George and Jesse told the army that their last name was "Hill." I decided my last name could be "Ridge," after our rocky ridge. So the preacher wrote a "Letter of Recommendation for Ned Ridge to be a teacher at the Two Trails Crossing School."

Preacher Jones said I needed to "look presentable," so he lent me a new white shirt and new black pants. And he sent me to the barber with a nickel.

I walked for four days to get to Birmingham. Endless walking on endless roads. Then land flattened out as I left the ridges and valleys, and the road got busier. I talked to no one, just kept walking. The first night I stayed with people Will knew, sleeping in their barn. The second night, the house of Will's friends was abandoned. I was exhausted with no place to go, so I slept there in a shed, wondering what became of that family? Were they hidden Indians who got found out? I left before dawn the next day.

As the sun set on the night before the teachers meeting, I got to the edge of Birmingham. There were no longer farms, just houses and stores. I was greatly relieved to find the house of Will's friends. I ate a delicious dinner with them, and took a sponge bath at their pump. Got a good nights sleep in a real bed, and the next morning, I put on my new shirt and pants.

Birmingham, a big bustling city. The trees and fields had disappeared. There were people everywhere, running, walking, talking. Horses pulling wagons or carriages, mangy dogs fighting with each other. It was early morning, but the air already reeked of horse droppings and garbage. Made me thankful I was a country boy.

I found the big building where the teachers were going to meet. There was a big man sitting in the doorway. Taking Preacher Jones' Letter of Recommendation out of my pocket, I climbed up the steps. The man asked me to write down my name, and I wrote it down on his piece of paper.

I told him, "I am interested in teaching at the new school in

Two Trails Crossing." Past the man, I could see teachers chatting with each other, books and papers in their hands. It looked exciting, I wanted to be in there with them.

But the man said, "Two Trails Crossing is a 'white' school. You are colored."

"Excuse me?" I said, trying to remain polite.

"There," he said, pointing down at the paper on the table. I looked down where I had signed my name. Next to my name, the man had written, "COLORED."

He growled, "You can only teach in schools for 'colored' children."

I stood there, confused. His voice rising, the man shouted, "Young man, I am telling you to leave, now!"

Another man, across the room with the teachers, scowled, and walked quickly towards me.

"Go to the Colored Teachers Meeting! Here is the address," said the first man. The second man grabbed my arm and pulled me down the stairs, back into the street.

My head spinning, my heart beating, I found myself in the hot steamy Birmingham street. That man grabbing and pulling me suddenly brought back the memory of the men who grabbed Spring at the farmers market. I looked around, needing someplace to collect myself. In the distance, I saw a cluster of trees, away from the city streets, and quickly headed for it.

The trees surrounded a tiny stream, and unlike the street, there were no crowds of people. Only one man asleep on the ground. I found a tree where I could sit and see nothing but the flowing water. I kneeled there, splashing cool water on my face, and drinking my fill. Sitting under the tree, I tried to calm down and collect myself.

My purpose was to become a teacher, but suddenly I was not a teacher, but "Ned Ridge, colored." I felt like a steer under the branding iron, branded for life. Why did that man call me "colored?" I am Chickasaw, and we are a proud people. I should go and tell that to those men. I took a breath, realizing those men could get me arrested for being Indian, or worse. Embarrassed and angry, I wondered what should I do? Should I just forget teaching and head home?

Was I colored? Never before had I thought about the color of my skin. I knew my big brother, Will, tried hard to "look white." That's how he could travel around Alabama and Mississippi to meet with other hidden groups of Chickasaws, without the violent white men hurting him. Will always wore a hat outside, so the sun wouldn't brown him. I never wore a hat, didn't like anything on my head. So I was brown, like my mother and cousins.

I looked at my arms. They suddenly looked so dark, and it meant I couldn't teach at the new school. The school where my nieces and nephews – all of them Chickasaw – planned to go! The people in Two Trails Crossing knew we were Indian, but they accepted us as poor white people. There was little talk about Indians or "mixed bloods." We were all shades of brown. If you look at people, no one is really "white."

Leaning against that tree, I started to doze. Then I woke with a jerk. I've come all this way to Birmingham, I thought to myself. They say I'm colored, so I'm going to go to that colored teachers meeting!

I picked myself up, thanked the tree, dusted myself off, combed my hair, and headed back to the streets of Birmingham. I looked at the paper with the address of the Colored Teachers Meeting, and had no idea how to get there. I looked at the people in the streets, all of them strangers. Suddenly I was shy about asking a white person.

Looking to the colored people for help, I picked out a young man, about my age and size, and showed him my piece of paper. He told me his name was "Jed." I told him my name was "Ned."

"Maybe we're twins," I joked. He was very friendly, and said he would walk with me all the way to the teachers meeting.

"What's it like to live in Birmingham?" I asked Jed, as we walked along.

"Hard for colored folks," he told me, shaking his head. "Gotta be careful. White folks can be sure 'nuff cruel."

He didn't seem to mind my questions, so I asked, "Are there schools for colored children here in Birmingham?"

"Yup, there's one."

Then he pointed to the church where the Colored Teachers Meeting was in session. I thanked him and he waved, and I walked up the church steps.

No one stood at the door to prevent me from entering the colored teachers meeting. Inside, there was a lively discussion going. I sat down at the back row, listening to my fellow teachers.

"We're supposed to all be 'free'!" A man declared. "Nothing much has changed since emancipation, as far as I can see. Black folk are still doing all the hardest work. White people are still beating Negroes, and getting away with it."

"Oh, now, Howard," an elegant young lady responded. "There are changes, and more to come. Why, way up in Washington, D.C., the government just passed the Civil Rights Act, guaranteeing us equal rights to accommodations."

"Oh yes, the United States Congress did pass a civil rights law," answered Howard. "And it probably will be just as ineffective as that Ku Klux Act that they passed four years ago. The violent whites put away their white sheets —but they continue to kill black folks!"

The men and women in that meeting were of many colors. Many were quite dark, others light brown. A few had long straight hair —looked like they had some Indian in them, I thought. They sounded so intelligent, so knowledgeable. They criticized Jim Crow laws for separating the races. They complained about how few schools there were for colored children.

Then an older man introduced himself as Mr. Johnson, and gave each of us a paper booklet with written test questions in it. Silence fell over the room. For me the test was not difficult. I was grateful to Preacher Jones for teaching me so well.

When I finished the test, I noticed writing on the black board, stating "Open Positions for Colored Teachers." I passed in my test, and walked to the black board to read the list. There were only nine openings in the whole state of Alabama! They were in places I had never heard of, except for the Florence Negro District School. Florence is a city on the Tennessee River in northwest Alabama, only half a day's walking from my family's village. I wrote down the name and address of that school.

As the room emptied out, Mr. Johnson approached me, watching me write down information. "If you want to apply to one of these schools," he said, "do it right away. The fall session begins soon."

I thanked him, and then asked, "Sir, do you know a place I can stay tonight? A barn? A shed?"

"Sure," he said, "Come with me." So I went home with Mr. Johnson, had supper with his family, and slept in his barn.

I made my way up to Florence, days and days of walking, and interviewed at the Florence District School for Negroes. It was a big school, compared to the one-room schoolhouse they'd built at Two Trails Crossing. It was for children ranging from six years old to sixteen, with four classrooms. The job opening said they needed a teacher for the younger students, the six, seven, and eight-year-olds. The school principal, Mr. James, introduced me to Mrs. Hopkins, an elderly teacher who walked with a cane. She asked me to read her pupils a story. I sat down cross-legged on the floor, and read them stories. I stayed with her in that classroom for the rest of the day, helping her. I remember giving a lesson about the letter "p," with all those vegetables that begin with the "p" sound: potatoes, peas, pumpkins, persimmons, peanuts, pecans. It was fun, and Mrs. Hopkins seemed to like my teaching. At the end of the day, the principal asked me to come back the following Monday, a week away. So I walked for half a day to our village.

Six days later, I walked back to Florence. The principal offered me the job as an assistant to Mrs. Hopkins. If it worked out, he told me, I would get the full teacher job when she retired. Mrs. Hopkins was very happy I took the job as her assistant. She said there were many teachers who applied for the job, and she tried them out in her classroom. Then she told the principal, "I want that Indian boy." Mrs. Hopkins told me that her father was part Cherokee. But more important, she said, was the way I worked with the children.

As Mrs. Hopkins' assistant, I learned a lot. But only a few weeks later, she fell on her walk home, and could no longer teach. Suddenly I had her job, a full teacher job! I was on my own in that classroom with fifteen young children. That was hard.

I loved teaching, but I was lonely. I worked all day, and spent every evening by myself in my room at Brown's Boarding House. The other teachers and students were all Negroes, and so were all the people at the boarding house. They told me about the "Jim Crow" laws that separated the races. They advised me to stay clear of white folks, to stay in the colored section of the town. They told me places I could—and couldn't—go in Florence, where it's safe, where it's dangerous.

Homesick, I walked back to our village every Saturday, staying with my mama, going to Preacher Jones' church, and then walking back to Florence. It made me so sad—I wanted that job in the Two Trails Crossing school. I wanted to teach my cousins, and the children I knew so well. I wanted to live in our village! I was jealous of everybody, especially of Will because he passed for white even though he was an Indian chief!

I was angry at Preacher Jones for not warning me about Jim Crow. When I told the Preacher what had happened, he wanted me to go back to Birmingham to tell them I was not "colored!" I would not do that—it would put our whole village at risk for being found out as Indians. Preacher Jones was white! What'd he know about Jim Crow? Nobody in the village understood what had happened to me, not even my mom. So I didn't talk much.

Those were hard times. But things have a way of working out. As they say in church, "the Lord works in mysterious ways." The teachers in Florence noticed that I was lonely. Principal James invited me to Sunday dinner with his family. He had a big friendly family, but I was shy, and I spent that dinner feeling awkward, out of place. The following week, Mr. James asked me if I wanted to go to church with his family on Sunday. "Yes! Thank you sir," I responded.

It's called the African Methodist Episcopal Church, located right in the colored section of Florence. It is beautiful. I loved that church from the moment I walked in the door. I loved the singing, I got lost in the music. I joined the choir. Some of the gospel songs are the same ones I learned at Preacher Jones' church. Others were new to me, spirituals coming out of slavery. Some are sad songs of loss, and when we sing them, they take me back to this village. The joyful songs make me feel part of my new friends in Florence. Once I started singing at church, I made friends. That made it easier to live up there.

Over time, I became used to being colored. More than that, I became proud of being colored. Turns out, many of my new church and teacher friends have Indian, as well as African, ancestors. We face discrimination, are paid less than the white teachers, and have to be very careful around the whites. It's hard to explain, but I love my friends in Florence. I am connected to them. They have become my new village.

Then the best thing happened to me. Two years after I started working there, a new teacher came to my school. She was a beautiful girl named Talitha, with curly black hair and beautiful brown skin. She and I fell in love, and dated for a full year.

I went with her to Memphis, and met her family. And I brought her to our village to meet my family. I introduced Talitha to you, Annie, but it was only a short visit. Then we got married in the African Methodist Church there in Florence. It was too far for our families to attend, but our "Florence family" all came, and it was a beautiful wedding.

Annie, I would like you to get to know Talitha. She was born a few years before the Civil War. She and her mother were slaves on a plantation in Mississippi next to the Tombigbee River. Her mama told her that she has Indian in her, most likely Chickasaw, since they lived along the Tombigbee. Talitha remembers that the slaves on that plantation were different colors – some very dark brown, some were "high yellow." Some had tight curly black hair, others straight or wavy hair.

When the slaves got freed, Talitha and her mama headed north, and settled in Memphis–part of the Chickasaw homeland. That's where Talitha got educated and decided to become a teacher. When we went to Memphis to meet her family, she showed me those Chickasaw Bluffs that protected our homeland on the Mississippi River for so long. And they still protect Memphis from floods.

Talitha and I share a love of teaching and of music. We both sing in our church choir and are part of a group that sings songs from slavery times, and folk ballads. I've taught the group the Chickasaw songs I learned as a child. Talitha loves to hear me sing them to our children. Talitha has a beautiful voice, and

*when she sings those sad slavery songs of her childhood, I feel like
I am with her on that plantation.*

*Talitha is my blessing, my guardian angel. Our three chil-
dren need to know the story of their great-grandmother. Your
story. Chickasaw Annie.*

*Annie sat there, listening to my story. Then, wiping a tear
from her eye, she said, "Thank you, Ned, for telling me your story.
When you left the village, I didn't understand why. I missed you
so much. Thank you for telling me what happened. I am so proud
of you!"*

Then we decided to get back to Annie telling her story.

Annie continued:

We are almost done. These days, I can hardly walk, and
my eyes are weak. But I can keep talking–if Ned can keep
writing it down.

We're getting to the good part–weddings and babies!

13.

Two Weddings

Two springs ago, Misty came a 'runnin' to my house. "Grandma Annie," she called to me, "Gus done ask me to marry him!"

Gus Logan is that skinny little boy we rescued during the Civil War. After the war, his parents, Calvin and Nellie Jean Logan, decided to settle in our lower meadow, just below our village. They built themselves a small farm right there. That's how skin-and-bones Gus grew up with our village young'uns.

"Come quick, Grandma Annie!" panted Misty, catching her breath. "I need to hold counsel with you and Grandma Wilma 'bout marrying Gus. It's the Chickasaw way."

"Misty, dear child, I don't do nothing quick these days," I told her. "But that is some good piece of news. And I do love the Chickasaw way. I'll be down to Wilma's soon as I can get there."

I crossed the stream, walked to the other end of the village, and joined Misty and Wilma, sitting in front of their house. Wilma asked me what I thought about this

Gus Logan fella. I said that I thought Gus was a fine young man, from a good family. Marriage was a wonderful idea.

Wilma disagreed, saying Misty should find an Indian boy. "Why not marry that Chickasaw boy from Mi'sippi?" Wilma said to Misty. "He fancies you."

"Oh Mama," moaned Misty, "It's Gus I love. Known him most o' my life. I met that Mi'sippi boy one time. I don't wanna to marry him!"

"But Gus is white," Wilma muttered, shaking her head. "And I don't trust white people. The Chickasaws are disappearing. Everyone in this village is marrying whites and soon they'll be nothing of the Chickasaw left."

"Well, some white folks are good! " started Misty, her eyes flashing, her twangy voice rising. "Chief Will trusts Gus' daddy enough to buy land with him so we won't get sent to no Oklahoma!"

This is true. Will and Calvin have been calling themselves "business partners." A few years ago, Will and Calvin found out that some big white farmers were snitching land from some Indians because "Indians shouldn't be here any more." Will, acting like he was white, went in with Calvin to "buy" this land where we been living for generations. Will, like the rest of us, didn't have a last name. But he knew that Ned had given himself "Ridge" as his last name. So Will put down his name as "Will Ridge." So now we're "legal," and no one can remove us, as long as we pay taxes. Now we own the whole ridge, and the upper meadow where our village is, and the smaller meadow where the Logans live.

I sat quietly as Misty and her mother argued. Exasperated, Misty looked at me. "What'cha thinkin', Grandma Annie?"

Took me a moment to figure out what to say. "I know

how Wilma feels," I spoke softly. "We Chickasaws used to be a strong and proud nation. It is very painful to see our language disappear, our dress, our customs fading away. Even here in this village, most of the talking is in English. And we dress like whites. But in our own way, we are keeping some of the most important Chickasaw ways — our farming, honoring the earth, living the way of our ancestors."

Wilma nodded. Wilma and I got along fine so long as I agreed with her. But, I was about to *disagree* with her. So I continued talking, looking at Wilma, and keeping my voice gentle.

"Wilma," I whispered. "It is unfair to put all the burden on Misty to save our language and our ways. It's impossible for one person to 'save us.' I bet that Mi'sippi Chickasaw boy you met once is already married to a white girl.

"And, Calvin is a good young man," I continued. "I love his parents, Calvin and Nellie Jean. They and little Gus, came to us during the Civil War, running from the Johnnies. Gus was so thin, I feared he wouldn't make it through the winter. We saved their lives, gave them shelter and care, and they've been our good friends and closest neighbors ever since."

I'd gotten Wilma's attention, so I kept talking. "I 'specially love Gus. After Spring died, he drove his family's horse and wagon all the way down to Market Town to bring me and Spring's body back here. Little Gus grew up with our young'uns, and he is best friends with Chief Will's son, Jason."

After a long discussion, Spring and I wore Wilma down. She gave her blessing to Misty and Gus.

Turns out this marriage was particularly important to

us because Gus and Misty planned to live in our village–the Chickasaw way of the man living with the woman and her family. To be honest, Chickasaw tradition had nothing to do with it. Very few around here consider Chickasaw ways when making decisions anymore. Many Indians, even in this village, hide our traditions, trying so hard to be white.

Gus and Misty want to live here because they know this is a good place to farm. And there are good reasons for us to welcome them. It means Misty will stay here rather than running off somewhere. And if the farming goes well, some more of our other young folks might choose to settle here.

After Wilma gave her blessings, Misty and Gus announced their engagement to the village. How we celebrated! We thought it meant they would build a one-room house like we live in, and join us in farming our community fields. But no, that was not their plan. Misty and Gus wanted to create a "modern American farm" in our village with a big barnyard with hogs and cows!

Darryl, Daisy and Wilma were very upset, 'specially about hogs. Eve and I were more open to Misty's plan. Discussions in our elders council became heated. Shaking his head, Darryl grumbled, "They say a hog is one third cat, one third rat, and one third dog. I never thought I'd hear Indian Annie advocating for hogs!"

Darryl's right. I never thought I would want white folks livestock around. I *still* think our old traditional ways are best. But we have to survive in the here and now. Misty is a lot like my granddaughter, Willow, living between two worlds. There is lots of pressure on our children to "be American" and leave the old ways behind.

Misty and Gus said they wanted to honor our wishes,

not "remove" us. They said that nothing they built would affect our houses and fields. Instead they want to clear some land for cornfields, and build themselves a barn and barnyard for cows and pigs, and a house big enough to raise a bunch of kids. Most of this new farm needed to be on the upper meadow, where our village is. Misty told us that the lower meadow, where the Calvin and Nellie Jean Logan live, is too small for their whole new farm.

After long talks with Gus and Misty, I suggested that Gus and Misty build their new house near our houses, so when they had children they could easily come see us. And, I advised them to build the barn and barnyard on the lower meadow, "to keep the cows and pigs as far as you can from us old folks who don't like them."

It is truly wonderful that Misty found her man—that same boy we rescued. We'd lost so many of our young people.

Giving up Willow to a white family has been a hard lesson for me. It probably saved her life. But, these days, with things looking up around here, I wished I'd kept Willow, and struggled through the hard times.

That spring was full of surprises: Misty, Gus, Will and I took a trip to Judge Jack's farm! Will set it up, saying Judge Jack wanted to meet Misty and Gus. But for me it was about visiting Willow—it'd been five summers since I'd seen my granddaughter. Been so long that I felt distant from her.

We traveled on the Logan's horse-drawn wagon. Will figured that a horse and wagon was the only way that I, with my aches and pains, could get there. We left early in the morning. Gus driving the horse, and Misty, Will, and me sitting on the wagon bench behind him. We were in our Sunday best. Midday we arrived at Judge Jack's farm. The big house looked bedraggled. Paint had peeled off the walls, and the porch floor had holes in it. Looked like hard times since my last visit.

Sitting in a rocking chair on the porch, Judge Jack's hand trembled as he beckoned to us. I was surprised that he didn't get up to greet us. He had been such a vigorous man. As we stepped up on the porch, I saw how feeble he looked. Jack gently took my hand, telling me Willow was in the kitchen, and I should join her there.

As I headed to the kitchen, I heard Jack say, "So this is the Misty and Gus that Will told me about? Will and I discovered that we are cousins from way back when this was the Chickasaw Nation. I want to welcome you to this part of the family!"

I found Willow in the kitchen, pouring tea for us in dainty porcelain teacups. She looked tired and nervous, older than her eighteen years. We sat down at the kitchen table. She wiped her eyes and blew her nose.

"It's been hard," she whispered. "Grandpa Jack is sickly, and I don't think he'll be with us much longer. His wife, Grandmother Nancy, died about three years ago. They got married sixty years ago when they were teenagers!"

"Sorry to hear that," I said, remembering Jack's wife, who was sickly when I first met her back when Willow was a baby.

Willow lowering her voice to a whisper, "Not even a month after Nancy died, Jack up and married a young woman not much older than me! That woman's a floozy! She had a baby that she said was Jack's. Then she ran off with the baby – and our family valuables!"

"Oh my," I said, surprised that Jack would fall for a floozy.

"Grandpa's taken it hard," Willow continued. "He feels terrible that he's thrown us into poverty. And he loved—and trusted–that floozy. He seems to have lost the will to live. Now it's just me and Mama Rose, working to keep the farm going, with no money to hire someone to help us."

Willow cried some more, wiped her eyes. I noticed she had not yet looked me in the eyes.

"Auntie Annie," she mumbled, "I don't know what we'll do."

I felt anger rising in me, and thought to myself, I am *not* your aunt. *I am your grandmother and you know it!*

"Next week, I'm getting married," said Willow.

That took me by surprise. "That's wonderful!" I said, reaching over to hug her.

Willow started crying again. After more nose blowing, she whispered, "but William, my fiancé, can't know about us. He thinks bad things happened to this family because we were Indian-lovers. William believes the lies Rose and Jack told him. He thinks that Rose's husband was my father, not knowing her husband died many years before I was born.

"And I haven't told him different." Willow put her head down in her arms and sobbed.

Suddenly I realized why Willow was not looking at me – she was getting married and I wasn't invited to the wedding!

A wave of bitterness swept over me. No wonder I had lost my spirit connection to my granddaughter. In the years since I had seen her last, she had become even more white. And now she had a beau I would never meet, a man who knew nothing of her real parentage.

As Willow cried, it came to me that Willow had pushed for this trip—to say goodbye to me! I fought the urge to walk away in a huff.

It took me a moment, but I realized all this was much harder for Willow than for me. She was in an impossible situation. On the one hand, Judge Jack greeted my Chickasaw relatives with "welcome to the family." Yet my Chickasaw granddaughter faced a world where Judge Jack believed she needed to be white. And Willow was going along with this lie, even though it was cutting her off from her blood family.

Realizing this, I knew what I had to do. I reached over and touched Willow's arm. "It's your wedding and you should invite who you want. *But I will always be your grandmother.* This is a tough world, and you need to make tough decisions. I will abide by them. And I will always love you."

"Thank you, Auntie – I mean, Grandmother!" said Willow softly, for the first time looking me in the eye. We talked some more, and then she started crying again, and blew her nose once more.

She looked so much like her mother. When Spring was a young woman, she knew she was strong. But Willow seemed so confused, so weak. We Chickasaw women know that we are strong! Seems like these white families–even the good ones–teach their daughters they are weak. I remembered white women starving during the Civil War, because the white men thought women were "too weak to farm."

My sadness turned to anger. I gently lifted my granddaughter's face with my hands, and looked directly in her eyes. "You are a Chickasaw woman, and you need to realize your own strength. Don't tell me you don't know how you will manage. You have this farm, this fertile land. You have Rose and Jack who love you, and a man who wants to marry you. You can grow your food, raise your children, all right here."

Willow cried some more, so I repeated myself. Finally she gathered herself together, looked me in the face, and said, "You are right. It's all true. The earth is good and we know how to farm it."

Willow paused, then whispered, "I was so afraid to tell you about the wedding. After all you have been through, and all you have done for me. Rather than be angry at my unfair decisions, you keep giving me strength. I will always remember you, Grandmother."

Willow blew her nose, wiped her eyes, and then we got up. Willow took my arm, and we walked arm and arm into the beautiful sunshine of a spring afternoon. We walked through her garden and into the field, where we found Will, Misty, and Gus, marveling at Judge Jack's sweet potatoes. Misty and Gus had picked a bunch for us to take home. Gus went to get the horse and wagon.

As we pulled away, Willow called out, "I hope some day to come visit you."

Despite Willow's promise to visit, I felt like we had said our last goodbye. My heart turned from Willow to Misty–Misty who I saw every day, Misty who faced some of the same challenges as Willow. But Misty stayed by me. I was part of her life.

Misty and Gus got married that fall under the Harvest Moon. How we celebrated! Our whole village came to the Two Trails Crossing Baptist Church, where Preacher Jones pronounced them husband and wife. Ned was there, come all the way from Florence with Talitha, and their three little children. Local farm families were also there. We all sat together in that church, all of us happy in our different shades and colors.

A feast followed, with lots of fresh delicious food, served outside the church on long wooden tables, a wonderful celebration for everyone. I sat next to Talitha, with Ned and their children, and talked about how we may be related to each other through some of those Chickasaws who lived on the Tombigbee.

As we left the feast, Chief Will took my arm and we walked back to the village together. "Grandmother Annie," he said. "I'd like to pay you a visit tomorrow morning."

"Oh! How formal," I joked. "Aren't you that little boy who grew up next door to me? I remember when you were knee-high to a grasshopper!"

The next morning I was sitting outside in the morning sun when Will came over. "I'm glad you are sitting down because I have sad news to tell," he said. "It's not something I could tell you yesterday, on Misty's wedding day."

Wiping a tear away, Will looked at me, "Judge Jack has passed into the spirit world."

"Oh no!" It felt like a punch in my heart. Jack had looked weak when I saw him in the spring, but he was still joking, laughing, generous to all of us. He had been a pillar of his family. And he had taken such good care of my granddaughter. His death left me speechless.

"They buried him like a Chickasaw," added Will. "Sitting in a chair facing west, right next to his house, in his family burial ground."

"How is Willow taking it? How is Rose?" I whispered.

"I went by last week to pay my respects. They are sad

but coping. Willow is stepping forward, as she must. I met her husband, who seems a nice-enough fellow, but not any great shakes as a farmer, or a handy man. Willow asked about you, and told me some good news. She is expecting a baby!"

My goodness – a great grandchild coming! I'd been so focused on Misty and her wedding, and the plans for their new farm, I hadn't been thinking about Willow. That night, after the village had gone to sleep, I looked up at the moon and sent a message to my granddaughter, "Be strong Willow. You are Chickasaw."

14.

"Happy Birthday!"

I'm close to done telling my story. We are up to the "birth-day" stunt Ned pulled earlier this summer, just after the summer solstice. He got the village to give me a "birthday party"–to get me to tell this story so he could write it down.

It was a sunny morning. Everybody in our village gathered outside my house, singing that silly birthday song: "Happy Birthday, Grandmother Annie! Happy Birthday to you!"

Then they said, "It's June 26, 1890, and your seventieth birthday!"

Ha! I thought, why do they think today is my birthday? I don't know what day I was born on–but I *know* it was *not* today! My mother told me I was born in early spring.

But here they were, all my living relatives singing outside my house. They were in a celebrating mood, and made me come outside and sit in this beautiful new oak rocking chair. Ben, my nephew, made it 'specially for me from the big oak that fell down in the storm last year. Maya, Chief Will's wife, sewed these cushions for the back and the seat. Oh, does it feel good to sit in this rocker!

People gave me more presents — such a fuss! But I decided to enjoy it. Then the little ones stepped forward, and gave me gifts they made themselves: a pin of bluejay feathers, two dangling earrings made from maple whirligigs, three corn husk dolls, and a hot dish holder made of woven reeds. Misty put a new shawl over my shoulders.

After that the village made a feast right here outside my house, under the big oak tree. The menfolk roasted deer meat from their recent hunt, and the women made succotash and corn bread. After the feast was over, people drifted back to their own homes.

Ned lingered until he was the only one left, heating up a bucket of water over the fire. I wondered what he was up to. When the water was warm, he took the big bucket off the fire, and put it right in front of me. He put my feet in the bucket for a long soak. Then Ned gently rubbed my poor old feet. Ah, that felt good!

"Birthday parties are for white folks," I said to Ned. "What's this about?"

"I wanted it to be an honoring ceremony for you," Ned explained. "But the children insisted it was a birthday party."

Ned looked sad. He's been sad since last winter, when his mama, my sister, passed into the spirit world. Since Eve's death, I've felt like a big piece of my body is missing. Eve and I spent every day of our lives together.

"Aunt Annie," Ned said softly, "I would like you to tell me the story of your life, so I can write it down."

"Ha!" I laughed, "Some birthday present – you want to put me to work!"

"It's not for you," said Ned. "It's for all of us here, especially the children, and those yet unborn. Think about it. I'll be back tomorrow."

As night fell, I thought about Ned's idea. Following in my father's footsteps, I became our village storyteller. I knew Ned was right, that it was important for the little ones to know our history, to know our ways. And I did not have many days left on this earth.

But write it down? Our way is storytelling. My father taught me to pass down our traditions through speaking. He said that when we hear the stories, and learn to tell them, they became part of us. This oral tradition is how we learn and how we teach.

I grew up speaking and thinking in Chickasaw. I also learned English as a child because there were so many white people coming into our land. But I never learned reading or writing. Ned was the first person in our village to do that.

I love my Ned. He grew up next door, and since my sons died, he feels like a son to me. As I lay in my bed that night, I thought about the way some folks use writing. I don't trust them. But *I do trust Ned*. I fell into a deep, dreamless sleep. The dawn woke me, and I thought, "Yes, I will tell Ned my story. It will be the oral tradition, just written down!"

When Ned came over to see me that morning, I was sitting in my rocker under the big tree. "I will tell you my story, " I said.

"Great!" declared Ned, looking up to the sky above. "We need to start right away, so I can finish it before school starts up after the fall harvest. Also, I can't stay here all summer. I promised Talitha I would come back to Florence every Friday, to spend the weekend with her and the children."

Then Ned took out a notebook and pencil, ready to write. I looked at his notebook. I could see that he had already written something down. "What does that say?" I asked.

Nick read, "June 26, 1890. The village celebrated Grandmother Annie's seventy years on this earth. Chickasaw Annie was born around 1819 or 1820."

"Wait a minute, young man!" I blurted out, "That is *not* the way it begins. Those numbers and dates confuse me. This is my story. *You must write down only the words I say.*"

Taken aback, Ned said he was sorry. We sat there silently, as Ned erased those words with his pencil. I watched a frown move across Ned's face. I remembered the night Ned was born, remembered him growing up. I thought about the happy times–and the hard times–we had shared.

Ned broke the silence, "It will be *your* story," he said. "I will write down only what you say. To be sure, every day I will read you what I wrote down the day before, so you can correct any errors."

"Okay," I said. "That's settled."

We sat there silently again, as I thought about where to begin. "The story is about our village," I whispered to myself. "I need to think about how to tell it."

Ned smiled. "I'll leave you to think." I sat there until the sun went behind the trees.

The next morning, I started telling him this *Indian Annie: A Grandmother's Story.*

15.

Chickasaw Eyes

Ned and I should be finished, but things keep happening – wonderful things. The big news – Misty had twins! She and Gus have been farming next to us, and they are hiring our youth as help. They followed my advice and put their cows and pigs down in the lower pasture. We can hear them "moo" and "oink," and I've grown to like the sounds they make. And our young'uns are growing strong on that cow milk.

We learned Misty was pregnant last winter. She got so big so fast that Sissy knew for sure it was twins. Sissy lined up, for the birth, the biggest birth expert in these parts: my dear friend Berta. Berta came up all the way from Market Town, and she and Sissy helped Misty with the successful birth of a girl and a boy.

The morning after the birth, I went to visit Misty. The new mother put the baby girl, named Winnie, in Wilma's lap and Danny, the little fellow, in my lap, saying, "Congratulations, great grandmas!" It felt good to sit with Wilma, each of us with a baby in our lap.

Happy as I was, I wanted to see Berta. "Where's Berta?" I asked.

"She's plum tired out. Went home with Sissy to get some rest."

My heart fell. I had hoped to see Berta. She had been so important to me all those years I was walking down to Judge Jack's place. It had been so long since I'd stayed with her. I *needed* to see her.

I chatted some more with Misty and Wilma, and then wandered home. It started to rain, so I sat in my house, feeling happy and sad at the same time. I missed Berta.

Then there was a knock at the door. It was Berta! She had a hopeful smile on her face.

"Can I stay with you a few days?" she asked.

"Of course! So happy you're still here. I feared you were gone on your way back to all those women who need you in Market Town."

"Oh no," said Berta, easing into a chair. "When I made up my mind to travel up here for the birth, I figured I'd stay long enough to have a good long visit with you. We've got a lot of catching up to do!

"Since your rheumatism set in," Berta explained, "I been scheming to come up and see you. I trained Casey in midwifing, and she's doing good. And right now, they're no babies due in Market Town. A good time to go visiting."

"Thank goodness!" I said, serving us some tea. "All my trips down to see Willow, the best part was staying with you, talking with you. Often times, it was painful for me to go to Judge Jack's place. I felt unwanted. You helped me to understand what was going on. All those years – you helped me keep connected to Willow."

"Your visits were good for me, too," Berta sighed. "You

respected me, you felt like a sister. Respect is a precious thing. I do not see a heap of it in Market Town."

"I'm giving you a whole big heap of respect, Berta. For these twin grandbabies and for everything you've done over the years."

"That means a lot to me. There've been times…" Berta paused, closing her eyes. "One time I found a man, unconscious, lying next to the road. I saved his life. And as soon as he came to, he treated me like I was dumb and ignorant. That's why I work with women. But even women can be hurtful. When some of them are great-with-child, they need me. Later, when I see them in the street, some are too white to greet me.

"But your family's different," Berta continued. "All of you. Will is such a gentleman. When I see him in Market Town, he takes my arm, carries my baskets, and walks with me no matter where I am going. And you, Annie, with all you went though with Spring and Willow. So hurt, yet open to me. You were honest, kept asking me questions, and appreciating what I told you. I felt like I found a sister."

Berta wiped her eyes with her hankie. "So, yes, I been looking forward to visiting you."

"It's been too long," I said, noticing how grey Berta's hair was.

The sun came out, shining through my window. "Lets take a walk through my village," I suggested.

Going slowly, we walked through the village, and I introduced Berta to everyone. All the relatives were excited to meet the famous Berta–not only because she had helped me and others through the years, but she had just helped Misty bring twins safely into this world. Will's family insisted we share supper with them.

After the sun set, Berta and I came back to my house, and sat outside watching the moonrise. "Berta," I said, "I remember you telling me about that brave woman who people called Moses, who led so many people out of slavery."

"Yes," Berta replied. "Her name was Harriet Tubman. She was so brave, risking her life over and over."

"You told me she inspired you, and that she would be proud of things you've done."

"Lordy, yes!" Said Berta. She looked around. No one was in sight. "It feels so free and peaceful here, so I'm gonna tell you.

"Back in those years before the Civil War, *I harbored a fugitive!* Yes, I hid an African man in my basement for days. It was the underground railroad here in Alabama! He escaped to the North, and I hear he's still alive. I was scared! I risked everything, my business, my house, and my life.

"My master and mistress, long dead, would've been furious 'bout me harboring that man. They had freed me and given me their house. I love that house – but their spirits are still in that house. Harboring that man, I was betraying them, and that's why I couldn't tell you when we was in my house.

"Slavery time is past, but it don't feel like freedom. But up here," Berta looked up to the sky, stood up, and raised her voice, "Up here, I can shout! I helped that man escape! Thank you, Jesus."

We sat there talking long into the night. Then went into my house and slept soundly through the night.

Next morning, I woke up thinking about Willow. Berta had bared her soul last night. Now was my turn. As we finished breakfast, I told my friend that I felt hurt that Willow has never come up to visit me.

"All those long walks I've taken to see her," I said to Berta. "It's hard for her to get here. But now that she's grown, you'd think she'd find a way."

"Willow told me about your last visit," said Berta. "About her not inviting you to the wedding. I know that hurt. Willow is trying to be white to get along with folks, to raise her children and be a wife to her husband. She is scared of being found out. Many people – including her husband – are sick with that 'pure white' disease. They don't want to admit to any black or brown spots in their ancestors. They get hateful in a minute. That's what Willow is worried about."

We sat in silence. "Willow and I are close," Berta continued. "We talk like you and I talk. Share our fears and secrets."

"Oh my! I almost forgot the special message I have from Willow to you. Willow made me memorize it, and I had to promise to stand up to deliver it.

Then Berta stood up. "Dear Grandmother," she said, standing in front of me and clearing her throat. "I am doing well. I love being a mother, and a wife. I feel strong..."

Berta paused, explaining that Willow told her to repeat this twice: "I feel strong. *I feel strong*. And, Grandmother, I know what I need to do. Thank you, Grandmother for everything. Love, your Granddaughter Willow. P.S. I still hope to come visit you one day."

It made me happy to hear that Willow felt strong. I didn't even think about a visit. I'd given up on that a long time ago, and didn't want to get my hopes up. A visit would be hard to impossible, with children to take care of and a husband who didn't know she was Indian.

A month later, during the Green Corn Moon, Will brought a letter from Willow, which he read to me:

> Dear Grandmother Annie,
>
> I hope you are well. I am well. I am hoping to visit you this summer. Sometimes my husband must travel out of town, and I hope to come see you next time he goes. It will be short notice, and I will have children with me.
>
> Looking forward to seeing you and your village.
>
> Sincerely your granddaughter,
>
> Willow

It was nice to get a letter from Willow. Then Will told me he promised Willow that he would burn the letter, so there would be no chance that her husband would ever see it. Then Will lit fire to that letter right there in front of me. As those ashes blew away, I forgot Willow's promise to visit.

Meanwhile we had other special people in the village. Ned, Talitha, and their three little ones were spending their summer with us. Wonderful times to have long talks and get to know each other.

Then early the other morning, there was a sharp knocking at my door. It was Misty.

"Grandmother – Willow is coming! Gus has gone to fetch her."

I sat there stunned, not believing Willow would come up here.

"Grandma," Misty persisted, "We gotta make a feast! Ben's gonna slaughter some chickens. The kids are collecting firewood. Maya and her kids are shucking corn and cutting vegetables. Will and Talitha are helping. Everyone's all excited about seeing Willow."

I got up and allowed myself to be swept up in the excitement of preparing a feast. But I still did not expect Willow to come. "At least we will have a good meal," I told myself.

Then in mid-afternoon, suddenly Gus and his horse and wagon arrived. And there was Willow with two little ones. She comes right up to me, gives me this big hug, and says to her children, "This here's my grandma!"

The whole village gathered around us. Willow introduced her little ones, William, age eighteen months, and Rose, age six months. She explained that her husband had gone to a meeting in Birmingham, and Mama Rose had gone with him to visit her sister.

Then Will introduced Willow to everyone in the village – aunts, uncles, and especially the cousins her age. Misty hugged Willow long and hard. Misty and Willow, both young women in the prime of life, both had lost their mothers. Now grown, they both had children of their own. In an instant, they seemed to become best friends, just as their mothers had been. Then Ned introduced Talitha and their little ones to Willow and her little ones. So many of us – all here together!

Misty took Willow on a tour of the village, as her new-found cousins carried her babies in their arms.

I just sat there, and cried with happiness. Willow! In our village! I looked out along our creek at the stand of black willows, graceful and strong, deeply rooted, just like my Willow.

What a feast we had, Willow sitting next to me with her children, my great grandchildren. Willow talked a blue streak through the whole feast.

"For years I've promised myself to come up here," she told me. "I needed to see you, and meet my aunts, uncles and cousins. I needed to see where I was born and spent my first years. See the ridge and the cornfields and the gardens. I had to come, it is my heritage." She cried, and blew her nose.

"It's been especially wonderful to meet Cousin Misty. We both lost our mothers, but thankfully we had grandmothers! You and Grandmother Wilma are how we survived.

"I love all these aunts and uncles and cousins, and the kids. And I love Calvin and Nellie Jean, who declared that they feel like cousins, too."

We had a delicious feast – fresh corn on the cob, chicken roasted over the fire, succotash, corn bread, and pumpkin pudding. Feasting with all our whole big family.

After dinner, Willow and I sat together and watched the sun sink into the west, as the little ones played with cornhusk dolls.

"I need to keep this visit secret from my husband," whispered Willow. "He wants to believe what Rose and Grandpa Jack told him," she said shaking her head. "But I will tell my children when they are grown."

Picking up a corncob her toddler threw on the ground, Willow continued to talk, "Grandmother Annie," she said putting her arm around my shoulder. "Some of us women can keep secrets. Remember all those stories you told me, when I was small, about this hidden village? I kept them secret all these years. Only person I ever told them to was Berta, after I got grown and we became friends."

"You were a smart little girl!" I declared. "If you had told your Mama Rose those stories, she would've made me stop telling them."

"Berta and I keep secrets, too," said Willow, "just like you and she used to. It's a precious thing to share something with someone, and know it will never get out."

"This is a wonderful day," I told her. "It is a dream come true – a dream that I was afraid to admit I had, 'cause it seemed so impossible." Willow and I gave each other a long hug, tears in our eyes. Then we slowly walked down to Gus' barn where he and his horse and wagon waited to take Willow and my adorable great grandchildren home.

After Willow left with Gus, I fell asleep in my old bed in my little house. I dreamt that we were all here in the village, just like tonight. And the spirits of my mother and father, my husband and sons were also here, looking alive and healthy. Behind them were our ancestors, standing proud – Chickasaws, Choctaws, Cherokees, Africans, English, Americans, people of many colors. And in the middle of everything, there was Spring with her clogs on, swinging her arms and stomping her feet, smiling, and laughing.

I woke up. It was dark. An owl hooted. I stepped outside. The moon looked down from high overhead. A group of deer grazed in the meadow. It was calm, peaceful, a tiny breeze ruffling the treetops.

I sat in my rocker, remembering the day. How fine my Willow and my two great grandbabies looked. Those beautiful little faces looking at me with those big, brown, and unmistakably Chickasaw eyes.

We are still here, I thought. Somehow, some way, we are still here.

16.

Postscript

Ned Ridge, September 1929

Annie finished telling me her story late in the summer of 1890. Two winters later, surrounded by family, she passed into the spirit world. She was seventy-three years old.

That was nearly four decades ago. Our family still lives up in that mountain; I visited them there recently. My brother, Will, and his wife Maya, died some years ago, but their children and grandchildren live up there. It is no longer a hidden village, because they built a road that winds up that mountain to allow tractors and cars to drive up to the high meadows. Our old log cabins have given way to more modern wooden houses, but otherwise the place looks much the same. Misty and Gus live in the house they built, and their farm is thriving. Their twins are now grown with children of their own, all of them farmers in the area.

In the years since Annie died, so much has happened in the world – industrial development, growing cities, and a big war they called "the War to End all Wars." We hoped all this would bring peace and equality for everyone, including us colored folks.

But alas, Jim Crow is more intense than ever. They passed

laws making it a crime for a person to marry someone of a different race. They call it "miscegenation," and it means Talitha and I committed a crime by getting married, and so did Misty and Gus! These laws make people afraid to admit to their children that they have Indian or African blood in them. We disagree. We honor our Indian and African ancestors, as well as the white ones. We are proud to be "mixed bloods"!

As colored people, we continue to face discrimination, disrespect, fear. Talitha and I are luckier than most, because we and our children got educated. Our son and daughters became teachers and secretaries. Sadly, they had to leave our home in Florence to take jobs open to colored people, and they now live in Memphis, Birmingham, and Washington DC. But we all get together several times a year to celebrate holidays.

Talitha and I continue to live in Florence where we find solace in music, a safe way to express ourselves and share our heritage. For decades, we have been part of a local music group, of mostly Negro musicians, that also includes people like us with Indians ancestors. One man who played with us became famous. He was W.C. Handy, known as "Father of the Blues." The son and grandson of preachers, he grew up in Florence, and went to the Negro District School. As a young man, Handy went on the road as a musician. For a few years, at the turn of the century, W.C. lived with his wife in Florence, and we shared music with him. Sometimes I hear echoes of our songs in his music.

Although we try to keep in touch with all our relatives, we lost touch with Willow, Annie's granddaughter. I last saw her when she came to visit Annie in our village, so many years ago. But just last month, my grandson was at a statewide colored teachers meeting in Birmingham. He had several copies of Annie's story that he was giving to people he trusted. He was surprised when a white woman approached him, and told him she was a descendant of Indian Annie. My grandson asked her a few questions, and found out that she was Willow's youngest daughter! She told my grandson that Willow was alive and well. Willow's husband had died young, leaving her with six children to feed. The family faced hard times, but Willow was a pillar of strength. She put her children to work farming, and they survived. Her children grew up, got married and gave her a bunch of grandchildren. Willow told them about her Chickasaw heritage, making them promise to keep it as a family secret.

My grandson gave Willow's daughter a copy of Indian Annie: A Grandmother's Story. Now she has a book to share with her family.

In these trying times, Annie's story remains important. It is a story of Indians who stayed here in the South despite the removal law. A story of lovers who crossed racial barriers to raise children against the odds. A story of living with earth.

Talitha and I used Indian Annie: A Grandmother's Story to teach children in the colored school where we worked until retirement. Over the years, I made multiple copies of it, thanks to our daughters' abilities on a new-fangled contraption called a typewriter. Years later, our granddaughter got a job at a publishing company in Birmingham, where on the sly she produced several dozen copies of Annie's story. Don't ask me how she did it; her boss never found out.

I am now a very old man – turning eighty this year. Writing down Annie's words is one of my proudest achievements. Indian Annie: A Grandmother's Story has been passed from person to person through the years. It is like a breeze through the trees, a ripple on a pond spreading outward.

About the Author

With ancestral roots in the South, Sally Avery Bermanzohn grew up in New York. She headed to North Carolina for college in the 1960s, actively participating in the movements for civil rights, women's equality, and ending the Vietnam War. Graduating from Duke University, she became a community organizer and later a union organizer. She was present at the Greensboro Massacre in 1979 where Ku Klux Klan attacked the demonstrators and killed five people. Her husband survived a bullet wound to the head and arm, and is still partially paralyzed. Sally, her husband, and their two little daughters relocated to New York City. Sally went to graduate school and earned a doctorate in political science, writing a dissertation that evolved into the book, *Through Survivors Eyes: From the Sixties to the Greensboro Massacre* (Vanderbilt University Press, 2003). Sally taught at Brooklyn College for twenty years. Now retired, she lives in Hudson Valley with her husband, cats, and chickens, and writes historical fiction.

Contact Sally at sallybermanzohn@gmail.com

65957324R10097

Made in the USA
Lexington, KY
30 July 2017